The Pirate Empress

WHITE TIGER

BOOK 2

Deborah Cannon

© Copyright 2015 Deborah Cannon

All rights reserved. No part of this publication may be reproduced, stored in a retrieval system, or transmitted, in any form or by any means, electronic, mechanical, photocopying, recording, or otherwise, without the written prior permission of the author, excepting brief quotes used in reviews.

This book is a work of fiction. Names, characters, businesses, organizations, places, events, and incidents either are the product of the author's imagination or are used fictitiously.

ISBN-13: 978-1514774540
ISBN-10: 1514774542
BISAC: Fiction/fantasy/epic

Cover design by Aubrey Cannon
Cover illustrations by Insima

Also by Deborah Cannon:

The Pirate Empress Series:
Black Tortoise (Part 1)
Azure Dragon (Part 3)
Vermilion Bird (Part 4)

The Raven Chronicles Series:
Raven Dawn (Prequel)
The Raven's Pool
White Raven
Ravenstone
Raven's Blood

Drey McFee's Close Encounters of the Cryptid Kind series: (Kindle Short Reads)
Crowd Demon
Lightning Snake
The Hooded Bird
Water Wolf
The Bigfoot Murder
The Loch Monster
Tunnel Terror

Elizabeth Latimer Pirate Hunter (Young Adult) series:
The Virtual Pirate (Prequel)
The Pirate Vortex
The Jade Pirate

Short Story Collections:
Wolfbird and other Stories
Tales of the Raven

For Aubrey

In memory of my father Dan Yee

White Tiger is the second part of Deborah Cannon's fantasy epic THE PIRATE EMPRESS.

Previously (Part one, *Black Tortoise*), Captain Chi Quan of the Imperial Army had returned to the Forbidden City after quelling the pirate uprising on the South Coast to fall in love with concubine-in-training Lotus Lily. A prophecy said that her future son would rule the Middle Kingdom and destroy the warring invaders of the North. Trained by the great warlock Master Yun she was sent to work on the Dragon Wall where her identity—not only as a girl, but also as the emperor's fugitive daughter—was uncovered by a jealous coworker. Lotus Lily, now known as Li, was caught and sentenced to death, but Quan and his allies rescued her and they escaped to the pirates' Waterworld only to have her poisoned by the fox faerie.

Now it is up to Quan, Master Yun, and the Warrior Monk He Zhu to find the magic that will return her to their world so that the prophecy that her enemies fear so violently will come true.

This is book two of the four-book edition that reproduces, unabridged, the tale of THE PIRATE EMPRESS. The titles of the complete set are: *Black Tortoise, White Tiger, Azure Dragon* and *Vermilion Bird*.

PART II: WHITE TIGER

CHAPTER ONE
The Suspicions of Zheng Min

In the rain-shadow of the pirate's harbour, bamboo-masted boats lay anchored. So, they thought they had seen the last of Esen, did they? Nothing, not time, nor magic, nor sword would stop him from wreaking ruin on Lotus Lily's rescuers. And when he found the girl herself... The warlord turned and looked about. Some sort of shelter used to stand here, but the signs were old. He followed a faint track through the jungle to the beach. At the cliff base was a shining jade-coloured lagoon, where fat shrubs grew clumped with white berries. Although the fruit might be poisonous, he was starving, and with a grumbling belly he plucked a handful and ate.

A crane stood on a rock overlooking the pool. A wall of stones showed in the glassy water beneath its one-legged stance. Shadows moved as overhanging trees shifted in the breeze, and a mist hovered. The sun penetrated the mist, exploding in a rainbow, and the remaining berries in his hand dropped to the ground. A giant bird with the head of a golden pheasant, the tail of a peacock and the legs of a crane split the water, and the one-legged crane was gone.

%%%

The day broke red as a New Years Day banner. Captain Chi Quan and Lieutenant He Zhu rode up from a grove of mulberry trees, scattering a cloud of crows. Quan searched the landscape, slowing his horse to a trot, and the brown and white stallion reared to a foul smell.

Quan shot Zhu a wary look as they approached the garrison just west of Datong. The lieutenant nodded, hand dropping to his sabre.

"Move quietly," Quan warned. "Something feels

wrong."

As they drew closer, their hearts fell. What once was empty steppe below the walled garrison was now strewn with corpses. All around, the trees and grasses were smeared with blood. And far away, Quan heard the mocking song of a Mongol flute.

The fallen soldiers had been stripped of their armour, weapons, and anything the Mongols deemed valuable. Their trademark warning to the Emperor lined the road—decapitated heads of Chinese commanders projecting from pikes. Zhu uttered Esen's name, harshly. The last time they had seen the warlord he was hell-bent on finding Lotus Lily and killing her.

A short distance away they found the garrison in an uproar as men dragged away bodies to burn. No wonder they had not attended to the dead left on the steppe. By the time they did, there would be nothing but bones left to burn. The carnage sent shivers down Quan's spine as he spied a palanquin by the roadside and soldiers in Imperial colours clustered in groups. Obviously, someone important waited inside one of the fortresses, and he reined in his horse to a trot. "Zheng Min's men," he said over his shoulder to the lieutenant.

Zhu answered, "He knows how to make himself at home when he visits the wall builders. I'll bet he's inside the fortress making himself a cup of tea while the labourers burn the evidence of his botched campaign."

Quan wet his dry lips, nodded while his sweaty grip tightened on the horse's reins; it wasn't safe here. "You must return to Beijing, Zhu. Go to Master Yun's temple and keep out of sight until I learn what is going on. You mustn't be seen."

"I don't think anyone will be looking for me. I think Lotus Lily's escape has been forgotten for the moment."

"Nonetheless, I won't take any chances of you being recognized. Go. I'll find out what has happened since we left. Then follow you to the capital as soon as I can."

Zhu was about to object again, but the stern look on his captain's face changed his mind. He wheeled his horse southeast in the direction of the Koi Gardens behind the Forbidden City.

When Zhu was safely out of sight, Quan announced his arrival by spurring his horse to a gallop. He stopped in front of the fortress in a flurry of dust. Zheng Min, the military governor, came outside, a teacup in his hand, to investigate the commotion. "Where the hell have you been?" he demanded.

"I have been fortifying the walls to the far west," Quan lied.

"Indeed? For a whole year? Do you have any idea what has happened in that time? Your traitorous lieutenant, He Zhu, and some unknown soldier escaped with the Emperor's daughter Lotus Lily. While I, and half of the Imperial Army went searching for her, Altan, Esen's baby brother attacked the capital. Fortunately, I had the sense to return and save His Majesty from that savage."

Quan knew the military governor was exaggerating his role in the Emperor's rescue, but he stared in horror as he learned of the rise of Altan. It was Altan who had left that massacre outside the garrison walls, and it was he who had attacked and looted most of the border towns, though thankfully he did not yet occupy Chinese lands—always returning from his raids to camp on the north side of the frontier—but it was only a matter of time.

"His Majesty has been asking for you. I sent scouts east and west along the earthworks to locate you. Why is it you could not be found?"

Quan scowled at the military governor's insinuations. "You didn't look hard enough," he said. "His Majesty wants his wall four thousand miles long. I travel from worksite to worksite. It's a wonder we managed to meet at all."

"His Majesty wants you to return to the Forbidden City

at once." Zheng Min's eyes narrowed. His thoughts were churning in a direction that Quan didn't want them to go.

%%%

He Zhu's reluctant acceptance of the Tiger's Eye had transformed him from an impulsive, fearless fighter to a cautious, holy guardian of the Taoist gemstone. What was, was; What is, is; and What will be, will be. He had no pretensions of changing anything or becoming a seer. And if his captain was meant to know of the child, then Li must tell him herself. Else Master Yun must be the bearer of these joyous tidings. It was no business of his. His purpose was to find the truth concerning Jasmine.

When he reached the Forbidden City he dared not show his face at court. He spent his days in the secret chamber behind the Jade Fountain of the Koi Temple, sneaking out only to search for Jasmine. One dark evening he dared once more gaze into the Tiger's Eye, and it opened almost immediately to a vision of the beauteous fox faerie. She was alone in the concubine's courtyard, staring into a moonlit lily pond, startled, when she realized she was watched. How she knew frightened him even more than knowing he could see her; and the gleam that fell over her black eyes sent ice like sharp pins into his heart.

"So it's true!" Her white teeth flashed beneath scarlet lips. "The one holy Tiger's Eye exists. Who are you? What hides you from me? I know you are watching me, but I can't see your face!"

As she rolled her kohl-lined eyes upward to meet his in the vision, he immediately covered the ring with his hand. Even the sudden appearance of Chi Quan at the doorway didn't jerk him out of the trance. Quan frowned from where he stood, blocking the moonlight, arriving in record time to catch his lieutenant, shaking, cross-legged on the floor in front of the Jade Fountain with a lit lantern by his side.

"What are you doing at the shrine in the open where any passer-by can see you? You may as well draw a target on your back. You were supposed to stay hidden behind the rock wall of water." Quan cut himself short when he saw the stark terror in Zhu's eyes. "What is it Zhu? Are you ill? Do you need a physician?"

"No. I need no physician. What ails me can't be healed by any medicine known to man."

Quan glanced down at Zhu's covered hand. "You've been looking into the gemstone again. What did you see? Is Li all right?"

"I've had no vision of her since she awoke from the sleep of the black poppy."

More than a year had passed since he and Lieutenant He Zhu had left the pirate junk. "Then what has turned your face white like stone?"

He had come to the Forbidden City to look for Jasmine. He had found her. "You were right all along," Zhu said. "*Huli Jing* is Jasmine."

If Jasmine was back at court, she would inevitably find her way to Master Yun's temple. If only Master Yun had left them the Scimitar of Yongfang: that blade would have kept Zhu's face anonymous, but clearly he had some other reason for wanting the ancient sword himself.

"Where will I go?" Zhu asked. "Jasmine must not find me. She will want the gemstone. And I don't know if I can resist her."

"You'll come with me. His Majesty never visits the work on the walls. If you stay masked, no one will recognize you. You can help to finish the wall-building. But you can't stay here." Quan's eyes narrowed. "I only hope Military Governor Zheng Min has tired of visiting the worksites."

Despite the suspicions of Zheng Min there was no other alternative, and on solstice of that winter Zhu donned his helmet, faceguard down to avoid recognition, and joined Quan and his troops on the border wall.

The next few months were uneventful, and Esen did not join his brother in a new wave of raids. Those who governed within the court of the Forbidden City sat safe in Beijing, trusting in Quan's diligence and in the strength of their ever-growing walls. Vast regiments of labourers were recruited to fortify the frontier's ancient earthworks with stone. For the most part, Altan was unable to smash his way though the several hundred-mile renovation covering the northwest approaches to the capital. Quan made sure every fortress was manned and every beacon lit at the first sign of the invaders, as his men continued to strengthen and lengthen the border walls. As a reward for his extraordinary efforts Quan was made Brigade General, much to Military Governor Zheng Min's disdain.

But the peace did not last long. Altan was more ambitious and ruthless than his brother. The eastern and westernmost points of their efforts were weak and needed further fortification, and until Quan's armies were able to build a continuous stone perimeter around the full extent of the Emperor's territories, and use every man in the Middle Kingdom to guard it, the Mongols found a way in at either end.

Altan knew all he had to do was to ride far enough until he found the weak spots. To the west, Datong and Xuanfu held because Quan's new commander there bribed the nomads into submission. The Mongols were starving after a five-month drought, and in exchange for food, they lowered their weapons. But by late September, the fields of the Middle Kingdom were ripe for harvest, and the crops and field hands were vulnerable outside the city walls. They were unable to defend themselves against the Mongol raiders. Altan drove his horsemen as far as the suburbs of the capital, and camped in Tongzou, from where he and his bandits easily burned and looted the surrounding land.

As a final insult, Altan led seven hundred men up to the northern face of the Forbidden City to bang on Anding Gate, the Gate of Safety and Security, ostensibly the triumphal entrance of His Majesty's returns from military conquests.

Panic and recrimination spread throughout the capital. As the city folk watched helplessly from the towers of the walled city, the suburbs steamed black smoke. In the countryside, the estates of the wealthy were laid waste, and as the months passed, every man, woman and child learned to fear the name of Altan.

His Majesty ordered Quan to return to court to discuss further military strategy against this new warlord, and Zheng Min was there to greet him at the palace. He was wary around the military governor, for Zheng Min still asked questions concerning his yearlong absence, hoping to trip him up.

"The people are complaining that we are restraining the army," Quan said. "The wealthy worry over their country estates and accuse us of withholding our full strength to save them from the Mongol hordes. They say we allow the invaders to pillage at will."

"Nonsense," Military Governor Zheng Min said. "We are giving them all the help we can."

Quan knew this was a lie. The new grand secretary had advised Zheng Min and His Majesty not to dispatch the capital's army. A defeat in or near the steppe, hundreds of miles from the city's watchers, could be translated at court as victory. A massacre below the city walls or in the nearby country estates was impossible to conceal from the crowds. The city folk must never know how near to annihilation they were, else they would rise in revolt. Quan thought a rebellion might be the best thing. But his fealty was true, and he knew that most of the ill-doings of His Majesty were really the will of the fox faerie.

At the end of the year, Brigade General Chi Quan returned to the westernmost extreme of the frontier where the defenses were weakest. This was Jiayuguan. Quan had four thousand men refurbish this portion of the wall, constructing sturdy ramparts and forts crenellated for weaponry. With that done, he left a sentinel of four hundred to guard the west wall and made the months long journey to the easternmost endpoint where he had assigned Lieutenant He Zhu.

Every day that Zhu stayed among the Emperor's men, he risked recognition and exposure. The lieutenant was no traitor and had done his part to reinforce His Majesty's great wall. Now it was time for him to leave and seek his own destiny. Wasn't that what Master Yun had told him to do? He was never supposed to return to Beijing. It was too dangerous.

By the time Quan arrived at Shanhaiguan, Zhu had come to the same conclusion. They stood together along the shores of the Yellow Sea, where the waves crashed into the rocks below a plaque marking the wall's end. It read: The First Pass Under Heaven.

"Zhu," Quan said. "Go back to the monkey country. Find the water people and look after Li. Reassure her that I have not abandoned her. I will join you as soon as I can."

"And Jasmine?" Zhu asked. "If she leaves our emperor's side and fully unites with Altan, what then?"

Quan looked down at the waves threatening to soak his boots. "I have no doubt she will throw in with the Mongols soon. Up until now, she was not certain which lord was more powerful—Esen and his Mongols or the Emperor and his army. She will side with those most likely to win and she believes it will be Altan."

"If what they say about her is true. She is very powerful."

What they said about her was true.

A shadow loomed from above them, one of the sentinels. But the shape did not move on, and Quan turned to seek the curved roof of the fortress crowning the thirty-foot-high brick wall. The yellow triangle with the green dragon snapped from a pole mounted on one of the corner roof peaks. The sky beyond the black form on the rampart was deep red. As it raised its arms, the characteristic C-bow of the Mongols stood stark against the sky.

"Duck!" Zhu shouted.

Quan dropped to his stomach just as an arrow whined by his ear, smashing into a rock jutting from the sea. Zhu had fallen to his belly, and now rolled to his side, crossbow at the ready, and took aim.

The archer stepped backward into the door of the fortress and blended into the shadows. "This is not the end," he shouted. "It is but the beginning! You think your puny wall will stop me?" He laughed. "Think again!"

Quan heard a whinny. Zhu aimed his crossbow, and a horseman rode out into full view. Zhu could have shot him right then, but something stayed his hand. This was no ordinary barbarian. A hawk flew from somewhere out of the sky, and landed on his falconer's glove.

Zhu released his bow too late, and the horseman was off like a shot.

CHAPTER TWO
The Nine-tailed Fox Kit

The monstrous barrier was completed. Finally, by the will of one emperor the fortified ramparts were linked into a single long wall dividing Mongolia from China, despite continuous Mongol incursions and five years of purse-breaking work. How dare they, Altan thought. How dare they think they could draw this line on the gods' naked earth. He stirred his horse with a kick in the flanks and raced along the north side, parallel to the wall. The solid brick ramparts were impenetrable; and towers punctuating the barricade hid watchmen armed with crossbows. Altan wheeled his horse, churning up dust and galloped back in the direction he had come. For miles and miles, all he could see was the grey-brown brick of the newly named Dragon Wall, its endpoints vanishing into mist.

%%%

Jasmine walked out of Altan's tent and went to the warlord who was passing the reins of his lathered horse to a boy, while the cries of a newborn blended with the notes of a piper's song.

"It's about time you returned," she said, taking his arm. "You have a girl."

He scowled, flinging dust and grit from his armour, and stamped his boots to remove caked sand from his soles. "I have no use for a girl. I need a son to rule by my side when I take the Chinese capital and make it my own."

"We'll see what your brother has to say about that."

"My brother is lost," Altan said. "He has deserted his men and the campaign, and for what? To chase down a prophecy. Lotus Lily is harmless."

"Perhaps, but what of the Emperor's new general? He is a man to be reckoned with."

"I have seen him at the easternmost pass. He had a chance to kill me and he didn't."

"Be that as it may, he mustn't be dismissed. He has a stout heart and a fearless soul, and he will not let you take the Empire while he stands."

"Then I will kill him."

Altan lifted the wolf furs from the entrance to his tent, and the notes of the flute followed him in. The infant's cries ceased as he caught sight of a half-naked young woman reclining on the floor of his shelter against red silk pillows and satin coverlets. A golden-skinned infant nestled at one breast, the nipple securely trapped between plump vermilion lips.

"Give me the child," Jasmine said. The wet nurse had lost her own baby to a freak accident when the branch of a mulberry tree had fallen onto the sleeping boy, and her breasts ached to be released of the pressure of her own milk. The wet nurse complied, and parted the wolf furs to slip outside.

"I never promised you a son. But I think you will agree, this is better." Jasmine placed the baby girl among the pillows and coverlets, and the infant crawled onto her knees.

Altan raised his hands, palms up, in exasperation. "I have no time to babysit. I have a campaign to plan."

From where the baby girl should have been a small golden fox kit suddenly scampered out from between two pillows, sporting nine flaxen tails tipped with white. She approached her father.

Altan shot a glance at Jasmine, and she placed her hands on her hips, which showed no signs of her recent pregnancy. "Your daughter is a fox faerie, my lord. And not an ordinary one at that."

On his haunches now, he played with the fox kit as she tumbled and rolled, her nine tails twitching, soft as rabbit's fur, and his flat, stern eyes stretched wide. "Then, she's like you?"

"Maybe, maybe not. We shall see."

"And you knew all the time this would happen?"

"One never knows everything. I knew it *could* happen. But as I told you at her conception, it has not happened in a thousand years. The last fox faerie with nine tails was Dahlia. Her power was great indeed, and she surpassed even me."

"What happened to her?" Altan asked. Jasmine's eyes shifted slightly, but she said nothing, and Altan lifted the nine-tailed fox in his hand. "She's so tiny."

"Most newborns are. What will you name her?"

"I will name her Peng."

"Peng is a Chinese name. A giant bird of great power."

"Exactly. One day she will be empress of all China."

Jasmine laughed. Of course. A summer baby, she was born under the sign of the Vermilion Bird. She might as well have a Chinese name.

Altan rolled his fox faerie kit onto the pillows and coverlet. "Call the wet-nurse. The child must feed." He lifted his falconer's glove from a corner of the room and strapped it to his left arm, strutted to the door, and then turned back to Jasmine. "If only I could see what the Chinese are up to. Do they really think their wall will stop me? This Brigade General Chi Quan seems to be a crafty advisor. If only I could know his true plans, I could break them."

"I may be able to help you there, but you seem to be doing pretty well on your own. Give me a month. I may find something to speed up your victory."

"If only I knew where Esen was," he said bitterly. "I don't want that maniac to get in my way." If his brother got wind of Altan's doings, he could become a problem. Esen was beside himself with rage over the rescue of Lotus Lily. He wanted her dead and was consumed with the desire to the point of madness. There was no telling what he could or might do when he learned that Altan had usurped him.

When Jasmine left Eng Tong dead in the jungle path,

she had travelled poste haste to the Forbidden City to learn what news she could. Esen had refused to go with her. After the fire died on First Emperor's tomb, he returned to the earth mound to search for signs of Lotus Lily; and failing to find her had hunted in the surrounding plains and jungles. In time, and disgusted with the single-mindedness of their leader, Esen's small pack of bandits had deserted him, returning to a new warlord, Altan—a man of fierce energy who made promises that he kept. For all Jasmine knew, Esen was still in Xian.

But Esen and his madness could wait. She wished to locate the Tiger's Eye. The memory of that eyelock, in the vision of the lily pond, told her that someone other than the ancient monk possessed it. She scowled at her inability to determine who that was. Whoever had that gemstone would have an advantage. There were three gems that had escaped the Etherworld. One was in the possession of Master Yun, one was in the tight circle of the Taoist monkhood and one was lost. These three gemstones were unlike any others of their kind, for they contained the essence of time.

The lost gem, a Fire Opal, revealed to the watcher what 'was.' The monks' Tiger's Eye showed the viewer what 'is.' And the warlock's Moonstone showed the seeker what 'will be.' Jasmine was not too concerned with the Fire Opal because that gemstone revealed only the past, and what 'was' had no effect on her plots. The Moonstone was out of her reach; it belonged to the warlock, and he controlled an instrument with which to see the future. But the Tiger's Eye: Altan would reward her richly for this gift, a stone that gave its master knowledge of what was happening anytime, anywhere. And it was entirely within her grasp—if she could find it.

The trip took her less than a fortnight. When she arrived in Xian, Jasmine transformed from a fox into a woman, and sought the temple of Master Tong. Another guardian had replaced him and she wouldn't hesitate to kill this one, outright. The monk was an acolyte, young and inexperienced. As she strolled toward him, he tensed his hands inside his long, wide sleeves, and moved to head her off. "No women are permitted inside the shrine," he said, nervously.

Jasmine stopped in front of him, thrust out her chin. "Since when? The last time I was here, I was welcomed with opened arms." *Among other things.*

The young monk hesitated. Jasmine could see that the acolyte was as unsure of this ordinance as he was of herself.

"Surely, you wouldn't turn away a weary traveller? I need rest and perhaps something to drink?" She knew she hardly looked travel-worn and her lovely white gown was as pristine as new fallen snow.

"I have only water. You may have that. But you must leave the temple at once."

Jasmine sighed. "Fine, go fetch it."

As the young monk left to pour her a cup of water, she surveyed the shrine. There was no one else here. The guardians of Lei Shen were solitary. There was also nowhere in this chamber to hide a ring. Jasmine went to the carving of the thunder god and began to run her fingers over the fine blue relief.

"What are you doing?" the monk screamed, dropping the cup. "You mustn't touch!"

"Oh for heaven's sake. It's only a sculpture. What I want to know is: Where is the gemstone?"

"What gemstone?" The acolyte rolled to his knees to pick up the spilled cup.

"The saffron stone, the one Tiger's Eye. What have you done with it?"

The acolyte was not as dumb or clumsy as he appeared. He whipped a sleek, sharp dagger from a pedestal in front of the shrine and warded her off. He spat a warning, raising the weapon two-handed, and Jasmine studied his bare hands as his long sleeves slid to his elbows, revealing ringless fingers. Satisfied that he was not the one in possession of the Tiger's Eye and completely undeterred by his feeble threats, she smiled. Then, taking on her fox form, she snarled and lunged at his throat. Her white teeth flashed, and blood spurted into the air as she ripped out his vocal cords, mid scream.

She did not stop to examine her handiwork, but glanced up at the clawed, bat-winged thunder god carved on the rear wall of the temple, and sneered. The blue-faced, beaked deity didn't scare her. He could bang his mallet to his drum until he was blue in the face. Oh, yes. Need she keep reminding herself? The mighty god was already quite blue in the face, and could do nothing to save the neophyte monk. Ignoring the carnage she left behind, she transmuted into Jasmine the woman, and gave the demon-vanquishing deity a mock bow. She was one demon that refused to be vanquished, and she went to find the brick crypt that she knew to be attached to the temple.

She found it.

So, the man Esen had pierced with his arrow all those years ago was Lotus Lily's beloved tutor, Tao. The eunuch lay on a stone slab dressed in a cloud-satin coatdress with a round collar. The sleeves were a foot wide and long enough to hide his hands, which lay crossed over his breast. On his feet were red burial slippers. The burial ministrations of Eng Tong, before Jasmine had made lunch out of him, gave the eunuch an eerie lifelike quality. His face was contorted as if in pain, his mouth frozen in a scream, unmarred by desiccation or decay—even after four years.

Despite herself, Jasmine couldn't help but admire the embalming skills of the monks.

Too bad Tao had not lived to learn the truth. Jasmine knew the truth, had wormed it out of Eng Tong as he begged her to release him from her ravishment.

The eunuch Tao was as much a man as any Jasmine had ever known, except that by the time she knew him he was castrated—by his own request. There were others in danger as long as he was seen to be a man. Well, now he was a *dead* man.

If Tao had the gemstone it would be on his right hand, but it wasn't, so who had it? Before she killed Eng Tong, he had told her it was safe among the monkhood. How had Eng Tong deceived her? If the ancient monk had carried it on him she would have known.

She shut her eyes to recall the circumstances of his demise: frost white hair, long monk's robe, but no gemstone. She could swear she had not seen the Tiger's Eye. Her smooth pale brow creased into a frown.

The scent of lotus blossoms was strong in the room, and Jasmine spied a bowl of scented water on a bench. The new guardian of the temple (or should she say the *old* new guardian of the temple?) must have left it there. Floating in the water were the torn petals of ivory-coloured lilies. *All right, then. Who needs the gemstone? I have the Sight.* Jasmine sent her gaze deep into the bowl.

Mind blackened, eyes closed, light bore its way through her eyelids until she saw what she feared to see: A small boy, whose steely gaze reminded her of a warrior she could not possess. She hissed and almost jerked herself out of the trance, but forced her mind to concentrate on the floating bits of lotus flower that returned to obscure her vision. The flowers cleared; the scene resumed. On the palm of the boy's left hand was the tattoo of a tortoise.

A voice called the name *Xian Wu*, the Black Warrior of the North, and by his side was the warlock.

Grains of sand started to fall and she knew the vision was failing. Angry, she scowled. Master Yun had defeated her again. The boy was born, but where was he? And where was the conniving warlock?

The sand reminded her of something—the desert surrounding Altan's war camp. Just before the vision vanished entirely, she saw her own little Peng snuggled in her pillows, and a hand bearing the Moonstone wielding the Scimitar of Yongfang.

The warlock knew of the nine-tailed fox faerie kit.

The gemstone would have to wait. She must find him.

She left the temple by the back way, switched into her fox form, and raced out of the village and over the river flats toward the lush green foothills of the Black Mountains. She never looked back. Perhaps she should have. As her fox's tail swept across the countryside, the dead eunuch opened his eyes.

CHAPTER THREE
The Bamboo Forest

Against the bulkhead, Li propped the rush mop that she had been using to clear the pirate junk's deck of seaweed and salt. She inhaled the crisp, sun-filled air. Her back ached and her knees felt like a dish of half-cooked sea cucumber. They had spent the cold season hugging the eastern coastline to keep clear of winter storms. Po wasn't kidding when he said his mother never stepped foot on land; Madam Choi had been ousted from her rice-farming family when she married a fisherman-turned-pirate. Rice farmers and pirates didn't mix, and rice was one of the main types of booty that pirates sought. People would pay an arm and a leg not to starve.

In a few minutes, Po had promised to take her off deck-washing duties and onto dry ground. They had anchored in a small harbour. The land was still frozen up north, but here on the central coast life was stirring. Green shoots coloured the landscape where bamboo forests flourished, and on shore there was movement, animals seeking food.

Li was now twenty years old. She had not seen Quan since the fox faerie slipped the black poppy down her throat while she slept. When she awoke, she was aboard Madam Choi's pirate junk and instead of the steely gaze of her beloved Chi Quan she had lifted her eyelids to the curious gaze of the sea gypsy's number one son.

"Are you ready?" Po shouted as he climbed through the hatchway.

"Is Wu still asleep?"

The stout young man nodded. "As always. He won't miss us. We'll be back before he has his rice gruel."

Li stepped forward to push Po aside, and Po put a hand out to stop her. "I want him to come with us," she said.

"He's spent too much time aboard ship. If he is to follow in his father's footsteps and fulfill his destiny, he needs to get his land legs."

"What father is that?" Po asked, sarcastically.

Li knew Po's feelings for Quan. What kind of a father would abandon his son?

Po sighed. "He hasn't come in four years. What makes you think he will *ever* come?"

"He will come when the wall is completed."

"The wall is completed, Li. The captain stays on the northern frontier to fight. He's a soldier. He won't come back."

"He'll find me," she said as calmly as she was able. "He will want to meet his son."

Li marched past Po and almost fell over when her knees gave out. Wu wasn't the only one who needed to get land legs.

She went below to fetch the boy who was sleeping soundly, buried in furs on a reed mattress. As she stared at his sweet little face, she glimpsed a trace of his father's smile, but she thrust the thought of Quan from her mind. Four years. And not a word had come from him. Was Po right? Had he forgotten her? Had he forgotten that night in the lagoon when she conceived his son?

Chi Quan Li Wu was born under the sign of the Black Tortoise. On their journey north, in the heart of winter, baby Wu was born in the hold of the pirate junk under the watchful eye of the water god Xiang Gong. On the tiny palm of his left hand, Madam Choi had insisted on marking him with the celestial sign of the north.

"Get up little warrior," Li said, poking her son with the tip of her finger. "We are going to see the Giant Panda."

Wu opened his eyes, yawned and buried his nose in his furs. It was hard to believe that this little boy was the source of so much conflict. Well, he was safe as long as he stayed among the water people. He would grow up to be a pirate like his godmother, Madam Choi. Li smiled at her son's sleepy face, hoisted him out of bed and dressed him, then led him up on deck. Po tossed Li a sabre and scabbarded his own against his hip. They never left their junk unarmed, and even though nothing untoward had happened in the years since Quan had abandoned her, Li was forever on her guard. She had a debt to pay to Jasmine who was the reason she was here, for Li demanded her freedom—and her son's freedom—and when she had the chance, she fully intended payback, which meant leaving Wu with the pirates.

She handed Wu to Po, who hung from the hemp ladder leading to the raft, then followed and took position at the bow, her son on her lap, while Po poled them across the calm water to the shore. Ahead was the bamboo forest they had seen from the junk. It was eerily quiet and only the wind rustled the leaves. "Where is the Giant Panda?" Wu asked as they scraped ashore.

Li held her son's hand as they left the raft and walked into the forest. Po had travelled the waters bordering the bamboo forests before, and many times had set foot on the fertile lands. He had befriended the giant pandas and came every year to read the earth, and although his mother was a descendent of the Emperor of the Five Grains, Shennong, it was her son who had inherited the love of the forest and the earth. Po raised his hand, and Li and Wu stopped.

Po's face was creased with worry. Something felt sour and he told them to stay put while he explored a small glade. Li watched with her son, from the periphery, one hand on her sabre. A rustle came from above Po's head, and he looked up. "Mao Mao," he said.

The female panda lowered herself to a nearby branch with a mouthful of bamboo leaves, and clinging to her back was a black and white cub, identical to herself. Po smiled, turned to Li and Wu. "It's all right. You can come over, but be very quiet or you'll frighten them."

In the clearing a few paces from the bamboo tree, Po

pointed to the munching pandas that were paying little attention to the intruders. "See the little one? You may name her."

"How do you know it's a girl?" Li asked.

Po gave her a mischievous smile. "I just know."

"Min Min," Wu said. "That's her name."

Po grinned. "Min Min, it is." Then, he shifted his gaze away from the foraging panda, the frown returning to his face.

"What's wrong?" Li asked, her hand once again returning to her sabre.

"The forest is dying."

She squinted at the green bamboo all around her; it didn't look like it was dying.

"See the flowers," he said, going to a mass of hanging blossoms. The white blooms hung from the bamboo stalks like horses' tails. "When the flowers become fruit, they will make 'bamboo rice,' then the forest will die. There comes a time when all living things die. It is the end of their life cycle." He glanced around, crouched and fingered the soil, brought a small bite to his lips and tasted it. "It is early for the bamboo to blossom, and strange that the humidity and nutrition of the soil should change so quickly when winter is barely over."

"Where are the other pandas?" Li asked. "Surely Mao Mao can't live alone. She has only one baby. Where are the others?"

"There are no others," he said.

A scurry through the undergrowth took their attention to the ground, and a trio of rats raced across the clearing and into the other side of the forest.

"The rats wait for the bamboo rice to ripen. Their numbers will increase fourfold when that happens. I have no doubt that this forest is dying. Mao Mao has waited for my appearance to tell me that this is the last time I will see her here. She knows. She will move on and Min Min with her.

They will find a new home, farther north." Po still looked disturbed. "The only thing that troubles me is that I don't understand why this forest is dying."

"It's an old forest, maybe," Li suggested.

More noises came from the trees, and this time Li ignored them. More rats.

Po suddenly gagged, ran to the other side of the glade, dropped to his knees, and vomited. Li chased after him, leaving Wu with the pandas. "Po, what's the matter? Are you sick?"

He coughed, tasted his breath. Something in the soil that he had sampled upset his stomach. Poison? "I'm fine," he said as Li grabbed his arm to help him up. "But the earth is not. Something is depleting the plants of their nutrients."

Her head shot up, and she suddenly looked frantically toward the pandas. "Where is Wu?" She stood up, screamed. "WU! Where are you?"

"I'm here, Ma-ma," Wu said, crawling out from behind the giant panda that was now on the ground. Min Min went over to Wu and the boy hugged the baby panda with both his arms. The baby nipped at him and he screeched and let go.

Li laughed. "Come here. If you are to become a great warrior, you must learn not to fear the bite of bears."

%%%

Sometimes the stone opened its eye to him; sometimes it did not. How did this magic work? He Zhu had no control over it. After leaving Quan at Shanhaiguan Zhu rode south to Xian and the Taoist temple to learn from the monks what he could of Eng Tong's gemstone.

In a small lean-to at the back of the temple he stabled his horse, then sought some grass to feed the mare, but everywhere the vegetation was dried and wilted. Strange, he thought as he raised his eyes to the cloudy sky; it had rained last night and the ground was damp, so why was everything dead?

He entered the temple to the most horrific smell of death and putrefaction, and turned his head. He gasped in a breath of fresh air from behind before venturing to the shrine. On the cold stone floor, in front of a fearsome Taoist god, were the ruins of its former guardian. Zhu knelt beside the dead monk, who had no voice with which to speak.

"Who did this?" he demanded, releasing his breath in a sudden gasp, gawping in stunned horror at the dried blood and carnage. An animal, some sort of sharp-toothed beast, had attacked the young monk. Zhu glanced up at the clawed, bat-winged thunder god carved on the rear wall of the temple. The blue-faced beaked deity haunted him while, outside, thunder rumbled and Zhu could swear he saw the carving of the god bang his mallet to his drum.

He Zhu covered his nose with the hem of his mantle, and turning his back on the stinking carnage bowed low, and then went to explore the inner chambers of the shrine. He stumbled upon a brick crypt attached to the temple. The door was wide open.

On a stone slab, dressed in a cloud-satin coatdress and foot-wide sleeves hiding hands crossed atop his chest, lay Li's tutor Tao. The skill of embalming with which the monks were extraordinarily adept made the eunuch appear lifelike. There was no shriveling, no rot, even though his expression was twisted, and his mouth open in a scream.

The sweetness of lotus blossoms hung strong in the room, and Zhu located its source, a bowl of scented water on a nearby bench. The dead guardian of the temple must have left it there before the attack and now the flowery scent mingled with the odour of rotting flesh. An inky ring showed near the bottom of the bowl where the water level had dropped from evaporation, and floating in the remaining water were the torn petals of ivory-coloured lilies. A flurry of ice chilled his spine like frozen arrows. *Jasmine has been here!*

His mind darkened. Fear screamed through him like

fire.

"She is gone," a voice said. "Your secret is safe."

Zhu stared at the man speaking to him in stark terror. Four years had passed since that lurid day. "Tao! You're alive? But how is that possible? I saw the arrow pierce your heart atop First Emperor's mound!"

Tao rose from his stone bed to a seated position. "I would like to think I'm alive. But I'm afraid things are not quite the way they were. You see…" He paused. He laboured to get off the stone slab, but every time he attempted to stand, he fell to the floor. "It seems I cannot leave this crypt by day. Heaven knows I have tried. It's up to you, Zhu. You must find Lotus Lily and protect her and her son."

"You know about the child?"

Tao nodded. "Where the fox faerie is near, the Mongols are nearer. Esen has been here, too. But he was too cowardly to enter the crypt."

"He killed the young monk?"

"No, that was Jasmine. Esen came weeks ago, and has not left the vicinity. I can sense when he walks past the temple, too terrified to enter."

"Good," Zhu said, "then you are safe."

"I'm in no danger," Tao said. "Esen cannot kill me again."

Zhu's mouth dropped open. "What do you mean?"

"I mean that I cannot leave this crypt in the daylight. But come night, I will walk again."

What was the eunuch telling him? That he was a hopping corpse? Zhu stepped back, terror overwhelming his joy at discovering Lotus Lily's tutor alive. Tao raised his hand as Zhu unsheathed his sabre.

"Rest easy, young soldier. You are not food for an undead teacher." Tao pointed to the sword. "Even if you were, you could not kill me with that."

Zhu swallowed, staring suspiciously at Tao's perfect

features and re-sheathed his sabre. Beneath the eunuch's burial robes, was there a black hole where the Mongol arrow had entered his chest? "I thought the hopping corpse was a myth, and yet your flesh is not rotting and green, nor are you stiff with the rigor mortis. And how have you managed to remain in this state all this time if you do not feast on the blood of the living?"

Tao laughed. "Myths indeed. More like wholesale inventions." He swung his legs to the side of the stone slab, but did not rise. "I was raised with the Taoist monks. Even before this—" He glanced down at his half-living body. "Even before this life change, I fed exclusively on vegetables and grains. When Esen thought fit to end my life, I became what you see now and I learned to live off the life essence of plants. I would never harm a living creature, but neither do I wish to remain in this state. At nightfall, I must feed. When I take their life force, the plants wither and die."

Zhu sent a wary glance to the outer temple. "And the acolyte, the young monk, did he know of your existence?"

"I was careful not to let him know."

"Then why me? Why are you letting *me* know?"

"Because I need your help." Tao's left hand went to his right. "I had a ring, a saffron gemstone. I need you to help me find it."

Zhu narrowed his eyes suspiciously. "Why?"

Tao stared Zhu in the face. "You and Quan took Lotus Lily to a safe place. Is she still there?"

"Perhaps."

"It may be time that you moved her. As you have seen from the butchery in Lei Shen's shrine, Jasmine has been here. She will stop at nothing until she brings down the Empire. So far, she is on the wrong track and I'm hoping she will seek Master Yun, which will take her far away from Li. But Esen is not so easily led, and he blames Lotus Lily for the collapse of his leadership. He has gone mad, and will hunt her down and kill her son."

"He won't find her," Zhu said. "No one knows where she is. Not even Quan. She is in the safekeeping of the water people, and you know how slippery they are. They come and go as they please. They will not be found if they don't want to be."

"Good," Tao said. "But I still need you to help me find the Tiger's Eye."

Zhu could barely contain his breath or his heart from beating so hard.

"What is it, Lieutenant? Is there something you want to tell me?"

His right hand was hidden under his mantle, and he hesitated, and then looked up to see Tao's recriminating stare. "How did you come to be this way? I have seen death a thousandfold and never have I seen a soldier rise after an arrow pierced his heart."

"I knew I should not have deserted your training," Tao said under his breath.

What training? Why on earth should a palace eunuch have anything to do with training a Ming warrior?

"You have the gemstone, don't you, Zhu?" Zhu's eyebrows shot up and Tao nodded. "It's all right. Eng Tong is dead. I can feel it. And somehow the gemstone fell into your possession. Which is exactly where it belongs."

"How did you know?"

"Never mind how I know. I know many things. I was among the monkhood before I went to the palace." Tao pinched his lips together, looked Zhu solidly in the eye. "You are right in what you think. I am a hopping corpse. I was made this way because my soul refused to leave my body when I was killed. The reason my soul is not free is because my death was wrong and so you see me as I am, a being who is and isn't. I cannot even enter the Etherworld because my work is not done."

"You want the gemstone back!"

"Only for a short time."

"No," Zhu said.

"You do not trust me?"

"Of course I don't trust you. Listen to yourself. Listen to what you just told me. A hopping corpse!"

"If you do not give me the gemstone, Lotus Lily will be found."

"You're crazy. If I give you the gemstone, then she *might* be found. But as long as I have it, no one can see where she hides!"

"Zhu," Tao sighed. "If only I could have taught you myself. Perhaps this impulsive, stubborn streak in you would have been annihilated."

Tao's cryptic insinuations made Zhu nervous. "I'm leaving now. Don't try to follow me. I will kill you if I have to."

He Zhu fled the crypt, and stormed past the corpse below the carving of the thunder god. The stench in here was unbearable. He looked back only once before he exited the temple, slamming the wooden doors shut, hoping that some other member of the sect would come and clean up the mess.

He was stunned and confused beyond help. He blinked his eyes several times. *Am I hallucinating?* When was the last time he had eaten or drank? Then he thought of his horse. The poor mare needed watering and feed. He searched for some grass or weeds or anything she could eat, but everything was dead and brown.

Zhu reached his horse and stroked her tangled mane. He looked farther afield and now it all seemed so strange. Everywhere within eyes' reach was brown and withered. Had the dead eunuch told him the truth? He shut his eyes, disgusted with himself. He had just called the eunuch dead. If he was dead, how could he possibly have spent the last hour speaking with him?

CHAPTER FOUR
Will-o'-the-wisp

When spring became summer Li, Wu and Po returned to the bamboo forest. It did not take long to see that all was not well. Mao Mao and her baby were gone. The bamboo had turned to seed, making 'bamboo rice' to feed the infestation of rats. Li was sick of rats, sick of eating them and sick of feeding them to her growing son. What hadn't become seed was brown and withered, and the remaining live bamboo was old with fluffy flowers. In a matter of days, the entire forest would be dead.

"Well?" Madam Choi asked. "What did the earth and the forest tell you concerning our mission tonight?"

"Bad signs," Po said. "Death is near. But for whom, I do not know."

His mother shrugged. "We must eat. Make ready for tonight's raid. There is a small merchant junk heading south down Honshu. We will intercept it. Li, leave Wu with Number Three daughter. She is still too young to loot, but not too young to babysit."

Li had about an hour until sundown, an hour to tutor her son on the finer art of being a pirate's son. He had shown no inclination toward powers like Master Yun, but this seemed normal, as she had shown none herself until she was delivered to the water people.

"Ma-ma," Wu said. "If you have the power of *Gwei-huo* and my great grandfather is a warlock, why don't I have any powers? I can't spew fire with my hands, or make the clouds rain or the sea swell."

Years back Li had asked Master Yun this very question, and now it made her smile. "Have you tried?" she asked.

Wu stared at his chubby fingers, shook his head. "I can fight with a sword." He pulled out the small wooden knife that Po had carved for him.

If Wu had any special powers, they would come as hers had—when he was ready. He barely knew how to dress himself, and like her, he must first learn to protect himself by his wits. There were enemies everywhere who wanted him dead.

"Ma-ma I wish to go with you tonight. You must train me. I want to be a warrior like my father—"

Li took Wu's hands, which flailed in frustration, gripping the small bones until they relaxed. "You are too impulsive, Wu." His impulsiveness reminded her of a certain lieutenant, but that was a lifetime ago. "One day you *will* become a warrior. But for now you must do as Madam Choi tells you, for she is your captain."

"She won't let me do anything. I don't want to hide in the hold while you are out stealing treasure."

"We do not steal treasure," Li said, and steadied her voice. "You must hide from the fox faerie. She is looking for you. And the Mongol Esen seeks you as well."

That night darkness descended over the junk like black ink. Li sent Wu below with Number Three Daughter before returning to deck to prepare for the raid. Po and Madam Choi, and Numbers One and Two Daughters had painted their faces with green dye, and applied bits of bamboo flowers to their cheeks and arms to simulate mould. The greenish-white effect mimicked fungus infested corpses, and to cap the disguise they streaked their hair with rice flour. The smell of rotting flesh was achieved with a generous smearing of rat guts.

Since the death of her husband, one of Madam Choi's best ruses was to mime the hopping corpse. Villagers feared the undead pirates that haunted the coastline. Li was unsure if the life-force sucking *Jiang Shi* was real, for she had never met a hopping corpse and hoped never to meet one. But in the taverns and bars, tales told of the practice of travelling a corpse over a thousand miles. Families, unable to afford wagons to carry their dead to their homelands for burial, would tie the corpses to long bamboo rods, and when the bamboo flexed, the corpses would hop up and down. Madam Choi had decided that *Jiang Shi was* real, and she disguised herself and her pirate family as such to frighten their human prey.

It was almost midnight before Madam Choi's accomplices started up the coastline toward the unwary merchant junk with the Ghostfire in its wake. Li's senses began to tingle. *Hurry,* the tiny spirits whispered. Li stroked her sheathed sabre and crawled to the edge of the boat. The scalp beneath her topknot prickled. Shivers coursed along her arms beneath her sashed tunic, and she hurled her grappling hook and began to climb.

Several lanterns aboard the merchant junk were lit, and Li peeked over the rail to scout out their quarry. She turned to squint down into the gloom where the others awaited her signal, and she almost signed that there were no watchmen, when a dagger thrust into her face.

"What's this? Get a load of this," a watchman called to his mate waving the blade about, making ripples in the luminescence. Li moved out of knife-range, while the flittering Ghostfire bedazzled the staring men.

"Fireflies," the mate said.

"Can't be," the watchman answered. "We're at sea. The wind would blow them away."

Li stifled a laugh and flapped her arms to make the shimmering lights explode into new depths of brilliance. How many aboard this junk? Only two were visible. She beckoned to Madam Choi, who motioned for her family to move. Po started to climb, and his sisters followed. The man with the dagger gripped the side of the junk, peering down, and missed spotting the serpent boat masked by the black sea. Nor did he detect its occupants who were dark with green paint and rat's blood. He never saw Li at all. He saw only the magic of *Gwei-huo,* whose dazzling dance distracted the sailors long enough for the pirates to board.

"*Jiang Shi,*" the seaman whispered, backing away when Po emerged over the gunwale.

The watchman dropped his dagger, and his mate froze in the middle of the deck, mouth half-open. Li distanced herself from the men, while Madam Choi and her daughters appeared on deck. The pirate chief demanded access to the hold. The terrified sailors indicated the center of the deck, and with iron bars lifted the iron grate, to allow the pirates to descend.

Madam Choi and her family took only what they needed. Food. Rice, oil, soybeans, dried fish. This ship happened to be carrying silver as well and Po stole several taels of silver with which they could purchase what they needed at the next port.

They might have returned to their ship without casualty if not for the vanity of Number One Daughter. The ship carried the latest in women's cosmetics for the Ming nobility, and she pocketed vials of rouge and lip balm, kohl for sultry eyes, and hair gel made from the finest pine resins of the northland. One of the sailors, who at first froze in fear, suddenly regained his senses when it hit him that a corpse would hardly be interested in beauty products. In fact, why were they interested in edible commodities either? Did corpses eat? No! They sucked the life essence out of human victims. They had no use for rice or millet or soybeans. Except to count them. Or so the myths told. Hopping corpses were insatiable counters.

The sailor dropped into the hold and flashed his dagger, tossed a handful of rice at the girl but she only scowled and hissed.

"So!" he cried. "You are a hopping corpse?" He flipped his dagger at her and it struck, felling her on the instant. Number Two Daughter screamed, Po drew his sword, and Madam Choi's eyes burned with demonic rage. The wine and gunpowder cocktail she had drunk was overrun by a battle cry fiercer than any male warrior's. She hurled her halberd at the murderer. The man ducked. The pointed end struck a different sailor and collapsed him onto his back, splitting his skull open. The hue and cry was up. They had to get off the ship. Li leaped into the hold after Number Two Daughter who squatted by her sister. Li slapped her in the face to bring her to her senses. *Lesson learned*, she thought harshly. *Vanity can kill you.*

Li placed a hand to the victim's throat, yanked the dagger out, releasing the full flow of her blood, and threw it at an attacking sailor. Number Two Daughter sat paralysed watching the blood gurgle out of her sister's chest, tears glistening on her cheeks. "Get up," Li ordered. "Help me get her into the serpent boat."

The girl was so stunned she could do nothing but weep as blood from Number One Daughter oozed all over her tunic. "I mean it!" Li shouted. "If you don't want to join her in the Netherworld, get up. Now!"

The sailors were blind to her presence, and Li sidestepped as Number Two Daughter sucked up her tears and found her feet. Fire blazed in her eyes brought on by the need for revenge. A good swordswoman, she took over the fighting while Li dragged the injured girl out of the hold and onto the deck. No one tried to stop her because no one could see her. Stunned by the impossibility of what they *did* see, the sailors on deck stood immobilized. All they witnessed was a limp girl lying on her back, bouncing methodically across the deck, leaving a trail of black blood, a shimmer of living lights floating ahead of her.

Po and his mother and sister raced up the companionway on her tail. They abandoned almost everything they had stolen. Without their lives, food and silver were nothing.

They slipped over the side and into the serpent boat. Li willed the Ghostfire away to protect their location. In darkness, they fled by sea before the majority of the ship's inhabitants were aware they had even come. Li stared at the merchant junk whose name was imprinted on her memory.

Say Leng. Dead Beauty.

CHAPTER FIVE
Esen's Madness

Number Two Daughter would not stop crying. *Silence!* Li needed all her senses to identify what was wrong. She looked behind, but no ship followed. They had not taken enough booty to make it worthwhile for the merchant junk to make chase, and yet she knew something was terribly amiss. The figurehead of Xiang Gong loomed near, and a dark shadow moved beside it.

A Mongol stood at the prow of the pirate junk with Wu in his arms, a dagger to his throat, and Li gasped in horror as her son cried out in fear. "So," she said, mustering all of her courage. "You have found me at last."

"And I have found the little one, too. This one should never have been born. Now drop your weapons."

"Why should we drop our weapons? You will kill him anyway."

"Yes, I will. But I also want you." The warlord smiled. "You have bloomed into a very beautiful young woman, Lotus Lily. Get aboard." He turned to Madam Choi and her family. "You others, go where you will. I have no quarrel with you."

Madam Choi rose, rocking the boat. "I will go nowhere until I retrieve my other children."

"Take them. I want only this boy and his mother." Esen nodded at three girls standing by the hatchway, and Madam Choi glanced from them to the dead girl in the serpent boat. Number Two Daughter was holding her hand, and Li could tell that she knew her sister was past help; none of Madam Choi's remedies could replace the lost blood.

Li stood to obey the mad warlord, but Madam Choi shot out an arm.

"I can't let him take Wu," Li said.

If Madam Choi's black eyes could have darkened any more they would have, but she nodded, stood down, firing a scathing look at Esen.

The three girls prepared to disembark. The oldest had her hands tied behind her back. The next oldest, Number Four Daughter, was eight years old, and glared rebelliously, reminding Li of herself at that age: fearless, invulnerable and completely stupid. Muscles tense, Li sent a warning glance at Madam Choi. She had lost one child; she wasn't about to lose another. "Esen," Li said to distract him. "I am coming aboard now."

The glint of a fish knife flashed in Number Four Daughter's fist as Li climbed the rope ladder to the deck, and placed her body between Esen and the girl. With her face to the warlord Li wiggled her fingers against her spine, motioning for the girl to slip her the knife.

The cold wood of the knife's handle closed in her sweaty fist, and she kept it hidden as she ordered the girls to leave.

"Wait! Show me your hands," Esen commanded.

"Jump, girls!" Li shouted. The younger ones helped their manacled sister overboard, and they landed in the arms of their mother and brother.

Li took aim, but before she could act, the warlord crumpled to the deck. Wu tumbled out of his arms, the Mongol's dagger falling with him, and raced to Li. She scooped him up—but it wasn't she who had caused Esen to collapse in convulsions. She didn't care who had; she wanted him dead, and flung her fish knife into the dark in the direction of his thrashing. But it stopped midflight, with a loud *ping*, striking metal.

She placed Wu onto his feet on the deck and told him to stay put.

A shield lowered, and the man behind it kicked both blades out of reach, before resting his shield against the cabin's bulkhead. He smiled. "Lotus Lily, you are a lost cause. Remind me tomorrow to teach you how to walk like a lady."

Li clapped a hand over her mouth nearly collapsing with joy as the impossible dawned on her. "Tao! You're alive!"

Tao glanced at the black, moonless sky. On the horizon a grey light sat on the edge of the world. "I don't have much time. I've come to warn that Jasmine still seeks you. Somehow she got wind that her plot to poison you failed."

"But why did you stop me from killing Esen? It is he who wants me dead."

"Esen is harmless now. He has lost his voice and his power. No one follows him. The Mongols have a new leader."

"Altan," Li said instantly. "But I still want his brother gone. As long as he lives he will try to murder my son." She gestured for Wu to approach, and he came boldly to stand before Li's former tutor. "Wu, this is Tao. He is a great teacher."

Tao hoisted his brows mischievously, and said with a sardonic smile, "So, now I am a great teacher?"

"The tea ceremonies were necessary. I realize that now."

"And this little one," Tao said, dropping to one knee. "Who is *your* teacher? Who taught you how to disable your kidnapper?"

Li glanced in astonishment at her son, before sending her gaze to the thrashing Mongol. "You did that?"

Wu nodded. "When I saw you were going to surrender to that hateful barbarian, I knew I must do something."

Esen's eyes bulged out of his head and his lips gasped for air, unable to get enough because his own blood was drowning him. Li stooped and dislodged Wu's wooden blade from the warlord's throat forcing the blood to gush out of the open wound. Esen grabbed her ankle while he spewed red mucus from nose and mouth. She kicked him hard and he convulsed.

"Madam Choi," Tao said. By now the pirate woman and her children had boarded. She stared at him, astounded that he knew her name. "I am Tao. I am sorry to introduce myself under such unpleasant circumstances, but this man is dying and needs your help. He will be of more use to us alive than dead."

"How so?"

"Look at him. He is a broken man, eaten up by the need for revenge. When he is healed he will see that his enemy is not Lotus Lily or her son, but rather his own sibling and his lover, the fox faerie. *They* are his betrayers."

"How can a madman be of any use to us?"

"Master Yun's plan was always to use Esen, not to kill him."

"And where is the great warlock now? He has abandoned us to these invaders." Madam Choi took a step closer, and squinted at his odd appearance. "What is wrong with you?"

Tao gazed at the green dye and rat's blood on her face, now smeared to a mud tone. "I am what you pretend to be."

Madam Choi's mouth fell open and did not shut as Li walked over, one hand clasped to her son's. She touched Tao's sleeve. It felt real. His face was not verdant or fuzzy with white mould. His hair was not frosted with silver. Nor did he limp like the hopping corpse.

"You believe it, don't you, Li?" Tao asked. "I have been watching you for many years now. I can move with the wind. But only when the red wheel of the sun sinks below the black sea."

"You mean you can fly?"

"Show me," Wu piped up.

Po stepped up beside Li, shot a knowing look shoreward. "I understand now. I see why Mao Mao left the bamboo forest and why it died. It was because of you."

Tao dropped his head in remorse. "I'm afraid so. I never meant to harm her, but I needed the life essence of the bamboo to sustain my existence—"

"So that you could spy on Li!" The voice that boomed was not Po's, and everyone turned to look as Lieutenant He Zhu climbed over the gunwale and flashed his sabre at Tao. Below the pirate junk was a makeshift raft strung together with dead bamboo.

"Stay away from him," Zhu warned. "He reeks of danger."

Madam Choi scowled. "I do not care who all of you are or what you are or why you are here. My daughter, my number one daughter, Leng, is dead."

Li squeezed her eyes shut to control all of the conflicting emotions. That was the first time she had ever heard Madam Choi call Number One Daughter by her name. They must give the dead girl her proper due, and then deal with Esen. Tao couldn't possibly expect Madam Choi to heal the mad Mongol after the death of her favourite daughter.

Despite the shock of Zhu's unexpected appearance, Li grabbed the wrist of his sword hand to keep him from slicing off the eunuch's head. "Tao is not our enemy." She turned to Madam Choi and bowed. "The choice is yours. You have no obligation to save Esen's life. If I went with my first feelings I would leave him as he is, drowning in his own gore. But Tao says that he should live. I believe in Tao. But you must do what *you* believe. Po and I will bring Leng to her bed and prepare her for her journey to the Netherworld."

He Zhu was hesitant to re-sheath his sabre and glared openly at Tao.

"You made it here in record time," Tao said. "The gemstone speaks to you."

Zhu tucked his sword arm under his mantle, and scowled. "How did you get here before me? It has taken a month to reach this place by horseback."

Then he narrowed his eyes and turned his vision on the dying Mongol. "If I learn that you led this savage to Li, I will personally kill you."

"How many times must I remind you, Lieutenant? You cannot kill me." Tao softened his gaze. "Why must you fight with your senses and your will. Why can't you believe what you see? When have I ever harmed you, Zhu? When have I ever shown Li anything but love? Do you really think I've come here to murder her?" He paused again, his expression compassionate. "It is likely the Mongol followed *your* trail to Li's hiding place."

The face of the warrior-turned-monk crumpled, and he rethought his accusation.

"No, you are not to blame, Zhu. Something about the barbarian's arrival here is suspicious. How did he get here?" Tao went to look over the side of the junk and saw no means of transport. "I see only *your* poor excuse for a raft attached to the hull. Where is *his*?" Tao scoured the deck around the dying Mongol and discovered a gold and azure peacock feather. He looked into the sky, frowning.

His brow unwrinkled. "I would not believe it was possible... but... anything is." He glanced down at his own form, at his burial gown and his red-slippered feet. "Just look at me. I would not have believed my undead existence possible had I not become a hopping corpse myself."

"Then you are as vile as that foreign devil there," Zhu fired back, and slashed a second look at Esen. "Whatever *he* has done, whatever sorcery you are about to accuse *him* of, you are no better. All the stories I have heard concerning hopping corpses say they intend nothing but evil. They thrive only by killing others."

"And you don't believe me when I tell you that I do not survive on the blood of humans? You have seen the barrens surrounding Lei Shen's temple. Now look to the devastation that was once Mao Mao's home." Tao jabbed a finger to the brown, wasted shoreline. "Is that not proof enough? Your eyes do not lie, Zhu. I survive by absorbing the life essence of plants."

Tao waved the gold and azure feather in his face. "But that is the least of your worries. If this feather means what I think it means, and Esen has tamed *Fenghuang*, then it is vital now that the warlord, Esen, live. Madam Choi—" Tao swung to the pirate woman. "Are you only a pirate? Or will you help this man?"

%%%

Madam Choi agreed to aid Esen on one condition: that the death of Leng, Number One Daughter, be avenged.

"I cannot condone this bargain," Zhu said. "That one—" he indicated Esen. "—Should die. Revenge for the girl means the killing of Imperial soldiers."

"Only if they get in my way," Madam Choi said.

"They will surely get in your way when they learn of your attack on the merchant ship."

"Those sailors deserve to die. They killed a young girl who stole only to fill the empty bellies of her sisters."

Tao interrupted. "We cannot get involved in your private vendetta. He Zhu must return with me to Lei Shen's temple. He has much to learn of his power with the gemstone."

Madam Choi's eyes blazed. She ignored Tao's excuses and confronted Zhu. "You still have a debt to pay, warrior monk. Your life or the life of the merchant sailor who killed my daughter."

Li spoke before Zhu could answer. "The merchant seamen of the *Say Leng* will be on their guard now after our raid. The Emperor's men will have been alerted. No junk will sail without protection as long as we and the other pirates threaten these waters."

"Good, I prefer a fair fight." Madam Choi turned to the men in succession, and then shot a glance at Esen. "Do we have a bargain?" she asked Tao. "You leave me the warrior monk and I will save the life of this worthless one. As for you—" She directed her next words to Zhu. "You serve under my captaincy this one time and I will absolve you of the death of my husband."

Tao hesitated, nodded, while He Zhu stared at the ferocious chief of the sea gypsies. "Agreed," Zhu said. "But when the girl's death is avenged I will leave your service."

The warlord's pulse was weak and he was no longer convulsing. Bubbles of blood gurgled from the wound in his throat. Number Two Daughter went below to retrieve what medical gear was needed and Madam Choi drained his throat of blood with a reed pipe. She administered a salve, and then sewed the gaping slit closed with hemp thread. With a clean cloth, she wrapped the stitches to protect them from infection. Finally, she drugged him.

"He will sleep. "But upon awakening, he will be a raving lunatic when he learns he is our prisoner."

Tao looked to the sky — already it was lightening — and inspected the gold and azure peacock feather in his hand. "I'll take this with me. When I am sure of Esen's devilry I shall return. Meanwhile keep him under guard."

Li grabbed Tao's sleeve and he gently loosened her grasp. "I must go or I will wither. The hunger will overpower me and I cannot be responsible for what I might do. I'll see you again."

He raised his long sleeves until they spread out like bat wings, the wind caught, flapping the fabric of his robes, and then he was gone.

%%%

Number One Daughter's burial was a simple one at sea. She was dressed in Madam Choi's finest clothing, which happened to be a paddy-field dress that she owned before her marriage to the pirate Choi. Paddy-field dresses were for peasant women of the Ming Dynasty, and to Madam Choi who had rejected fine gowns and robes as incompatible with pirating, this was the only finery she owned. Everyday women of the Waterworld wore practical tunics and trousers with sashes to hold their weapons. Madam Choi's paddy-field dress was comprised of a patchwork of brocades in various colours, and resembled a shaman's cassock; the swatches of cloth were earthy and bright, stitched in interlacing patterns to mimic paddy fields.

Leng had never looked more beautiful, hence her name: Pretty One. Too bad she had not known she did not need the cosmetics of the rich to enhance that beauty.

When her body was laid to rest at the bottom of the sea, Madam Choi sent messages to all the pirate junks nearby. They had been inactive too long. The smash and grab technique the pirates had reverted to after the death of their supreme leader was barely enough to keep the water people alive; it was time to reunite, to reorganize under one leader. Madam Choi decided that she must be that leader. What her husband had once accomplished, she would improve tenfold. The last raid she had attempted had been a fiasco. Not only had she lost a child and a working member of her company, but she had also failed to take the provisions they needed. Food was scarce, and over a meal of boiled caterpillars and coarse red rice, Madam Choi revealed her thoughts to her crew.

The only problem was that there was one man, a man who had always opposed her husband's leadership. He had only deferred to Choi because the other pirates agreed to him as supreme chief of all the pirates. This man was Ching. Ching might prove to be an obstacle.

Madam Choi and her crew returned to the South Coast where the pirate lairs were numerous. She called a meeting of all the independent captains to gather at a well-known opium den on the waterfront, and there, proposed her plan.

Inside the dark hut, Ching sat opposite Madam Choi over a pipe of opium. Unlike the taverns of the riverbank near Xian, here consuming the juice of the poppy was unheard of. Instead, the poppy was dried and stuffed into pipes. Smoke clouded the atmosphere and burned the eyes. But the men who haunted these places where addicted to the intoxicating effects of the opium and immune to its side effects.

Ching was dressed in a colourful tunic with a skirt that reached just below his knees. Most of the pirate men dressed this way, and only Li and Madam Choi wore trousers. In addition, Ching's head was crowned with a purple turban. His flat, naked eyes were nearly lashless, and lizard-like. Madam Choi did not trust him, and neither did Li. It was imperative that they set out some ground rules. They must revive Choi's original code.

Madam Choi requested that Li, who was educated and skilled in script, do the writing. She unrolled a blank scroll of vertical bamboo strips linked together with thick thread and handed Li a quill and inkstone.

"We are agreed," said Madam Choi, "that the first rule of the code be: If any man goes privately on shore, if he should transgress the bars, he shall be taken and his ears be sliced off in the presence of the whole fleet. Should he repeat the act, he shall suffer death."

All of the captains agreed. "Number two," Ching cut in. "Nothing shall be taken by a person for his own private use from the plundered goods. All shall be recorded. Each pirate will receive for himself, two parts out of ten. Eight parts belong to the storehouse, to be called the General Fund. Taking anything out of this general fund, without permission, is cause for death."

Li lifted her eyes from writing to inspect Ching's face as he finished speaking. Would he obey his own rule?

"And finally," Madam Choi said. "No man shall debauch at his pleasure captive women gained from shore raids and brought aboard ship. These women are for ransom only unless they choose to partner with one of their captors. To use violence against any woman or to wed her without her permission is punishable by death."

To Li's surprise, the pirate captains agreed. Madam Choi ordered a round of hard rice liquor, and they drank to the code before planning their first attack.

%%%

The pirates were out of practice. It was time to whip them back into shape. Every able-bodied man and woman must become part of a smooth-operating pirate-machine that made no mistakes. Number One daughter's honour depended upon it.

First up would be a plot to seize a ferryboat. The target was available nearby. It was a public transport that linked the two shores at the mouth of the Red River and crossed the channel twice a day. Madam Choi boarded the crowded ferryboat, and she, Li, Po and Ching mingled among the passengers, dressed as common labourers and peasants. No one was expecting a quad of pirates to be aboard, or a bevy of serpent boats to surround them. All went as planned, and only one passenger objected, while the cowering skipper hid at the helm.

The defiant passenger was, of course, He Zhu. "Release these people," he said, brown-muscled arms crossed over his chest. "They are poor and have nothing worth stealing."

That was true for the most part. What Madame Choi wanted was the ferryboat, but Ching insisted on taking captives. Most of the male passengers escaped overboard; the women were unable to escape because of the barbaric custom of binding their feet, and some couldn't even move without help, tottering rather than walking. It took all of Li's self-control to stop her fist from smacking these cowardly men for deforming their wives' feet.

Ching grabbed two women by the hair and herded three others and two children to one side. "Everyone else who doesn't want to be killed, leap off this boat," he ordered.

"They will drown." Zhu objected. He swung his sabre, which met Ching's in a loud clang, and Madam Choi warned him with a scowl that he still had a debt to pay. Zhu backed off, and shuffled the remaining passengers to the rail where most of them leaped off willingly. As the spineless skipper joined his passengers in the river, Madam Choi seized the helm.

One of the captive children started to cry, and Li reassured him that soon he would be home. His mother spat at Li, hissing, "Savage, cutthroat pirate. I would rather he were dead than go with you."

"We have no intention of harming you or your boy. Obey us and all will go smoothly."

"Over my dead body," the boy's mother said.

Ching planted his rippling torso in front of the troublemaker. Madam Choi had gotten the ferryboat underway and was steering the captured prize from the floundering swimmers in the sea.

"They will DROWN!" Zhu repeated, louder this time.

Li glanced away, every emotion in her body conflicted. "We need the ransom," she answered quietly.

"The agreement was not to harm anyone."

"No one was harmed. We aren't that far from shore. They will make it." Li looked overboard for confirmation and saw that the swarming serpent boats were picking up the floundering passengers. But the pirates aboard were laughing and bludgeoning the male captives with wooden clubs. "They're killing them!" Li hollered to her captain. Madam Choi shrugged, and Li decided to take matters into her own hands.

But the pirates ignored her command to cease the violence. The boy's mother who took the distraction as a chance to escape grabbed her son and lunged for the rail, but her crippled feet sent her flying to the deck instead. Ching went for her and she kicked, and screamed profanities. He dragged her up and when she cursed him again, he broke the top row of her teeth with his fist. As her mouth filled with blood, she kicked him in the groin. He got up seething with rage. As soon as he got near, she bit him with her bleeding mouth and with the force of her weight, threw both him and herself into the river.

They did not resurface, and He Zhu gawped as more of the hapless passengers drowned. He stripped to the waist and dived overboard, commandeered one of the serpent boats by throwing its navigator into the river, and saved as many of the swimmers as he could without sinking the boat.

%%%

"Madness," Madam Choi said, when they returned to the pirate's lair, east of the Red River. "A fiasco." She turned on Zhu who had returned to meet up with the pirates after saving the ferryboat passengers. "You have deepened your debt with this debacle. Your role was to pretend to be one of the passengers, not to save them."

"I will not kill innocent peasants."

"And yet you had no problem killing my husband."

"He wasn't a peasant. He was a pirate. And he was not innocent."

"He was a peasant before the Emperor's taxes turned him to piracy."

"Enough of this," Li said. "Ching is dead. Esen still sleeps on the deck of this junk and we are no closer to avenging the death of Number One Daughter."

Zhu swung on Li. "How can you go along with these ruthless plots to kill the innocent?"

"How can I not? Number One Daughter was my friend and my sworn sister. We did not harm the *Say Leng*'s seamen until they drew first blood. They had no reason to kill Leng. Besides, since when did killing offend you? You are a warrior. You have murdered more men than you can count."

Madam Choi stared at the ferryboat that was moored alongside her junk. "This discussion will lead nowhere," she said, turning back. "There is only one thing I can think to do. We must revise the code and get all of the pirates to swear to it in blood. No more fighting without permission. No more acting on one's own. And we still have four women and two children to ransom back to their families."

Madam Choi beckoned Li inside to write the new code.

Li sat with quill and inkstone opposite her captain, Zhu glaring at her. "Since when did you become such a cutthroat? Has life among the water people sapped all the goodness out of your heart? What has happened to make you so ruthless? You are a lady, Li, of the Imperial Court. A princess."

Li looked up from the fresh bamboo scroll she was unraveling. "Have you forgotten, Lieutenant? My father, the supreme ruler and emperor of the Middle Kingdom, the Ming Son of Heaven, ordered my beheading, and stood watching while his henchmen tried to do it. If that is the reward for a princess, then you can have it."

She jerked her head at the tattered interior of the leaky cabin. "Look around you, Zhu. This is our only shelter. Even a warrior like you never slept in such filth." She sent an apologetic eye to Madam Choi then swung back on Zhu. It had rained last night, and the mantle Zhu had used for a blanket was still wet, flapping just outside the opened hatchway, hanging from a makeshift clothesline. "How did you like your quarters under the open sky? Did you enjoy your supper of boiled caterpillars last night?"

"You kill for the wrong reasons."

Li slammed her quill hand onto the writing table. "Revenge is the wrong reason? Since when have you not killed for revenge? That massacre of Esen's camp at Red Salt Lake on the edge of the Ordos Desert; was that not revenge? Those were unarmed women and children, old men who couldn't defend themselves. Your soldiers raped and pillaged and raped again. And then they killed who was left. Pirates, at least, do *not* rape. It's against the code."

"I was under orders."

"*Orders.*" The hardness in her voice gave just an inch. "No matter right or wrong?"

"War is war. Esen's barbarians threatened to take our country."

Li directed Zhu's gaze toward the hatchway where three of Madam Choi's children sat in rags on the floor, their faces gaunt from hunger. "And this is not war? It depends upon whose side you fight, doesn't it?"

Zhu rose, his large muscles flexing with the movement. "Quan wouldn't recognize you. What has happened to you, Lotus Lily?"

"I have seen the world as it really is outside the walls of the Forbidden City."

Madam Choi gave Zhu a sour look. "You have much to learn, warrior monk, before you leave my service." Zhu turned to exit the cabin. Madam Choi took Li's quill hand and guided it to the bamboo scroll, and Li dragged her eyes away to dip the quill into the inkstone.

"You would do well to stay," Madam Choi said to Zhu's retreating back. "You might yet learn something."

He Zhu's rigid shoulders became powerfully still. He pointed to the hatchway where a junk approached by the eastern sea. "It looks like Captain Ching did not drown after all."

CHAPTER SIX
The Ferryboat Ruse

He Zhu stared at Madam Choi's unflinching expression. His original impression of her was correct. She was a slinking snake of a woman with a half-lidded gaze and a smile full of rotting teeth, her black oiled hair gleaming as brilliantly as her eyes.

"These women's families have no money to pay a ransom," he said.

"They had money to purchase a ferryboat ride."

"You are heartless, Madam Choi."

"What would you have me do, warrior monk?" she asked. "If I don't ransom these women, the pirates will insist that I sell them. I wouldn't wish that kind of degradation on anyone."

"You were better off pirating on your own."

"Was I? I lost a daughter, and Li almost lost her son. We need the security of a large fleet. And to keep that fleet together I must appease the men that work for me. That means writing a code they can all agree on." She turned her back on Zhu and walked out onto the deck to greet Ching who was hailing her from the quarterdeck. His junk was fastened to the ferryboat, which was tied to Madam Choi's flagship. The trio of boats formed a floating consortium. He was dressed in purple silk with a matching turban on his head, a uniform won from the lucrative days of looting the seas under the command of Madam Choi's husband. He was a stout and commanding man, despite the fact that his very presence grated on He Zhu's nerves.

Madam Choi bowed to her associate. "I'm glad to see that you survived the ferryboat debacle, Captain Ching. Welcome back. You are just in time to help revise the new code."

He had some raw scratches on his face and a bruised eye that matched the colour of his turban. Apparently, the peasant who had tried to drown him had drowned herself, and he had managed to swim to shore and return to his ship. For his troubles, he demanded a share of the ransom and wanted the prettiest of the captured women for his wife. Madam Choi agreed. "Now for the code," she said.

"Shouldn't all of the captains be present?" Zhu cut in.

"What business is this of yours?" Ching scowled, and turned to Madam Choi. "Who is this troublemaker anyway? What's he doing here?"

"He works for me, I want him present. Please sit."

Li prepared to write the articles of the code, but before Madam Choi could speak, Ching hijacked the proceedings as though he were boss. "Anyone caught giving commands on his own or disobeying a superior is to be decapitated," he said.

Madam Choi looked severely at him, but was ignored. He exchanged glares with He Zhu, and spat. "It is your fault the capture of the ferryboat went badly. Next time you will play or pay according to the articles of the code. Your death will not be mourned by me."

Madam Choi silenced Zhu's rebuke before it came out. Zhu scowled, but had the sense to refrain from further provocation.

"Number two," Ching said, again superseding his host. "Failure to surrender booty to the General Fund can bring death." That went without saying. Share and share alike was crucial to maintaining harmony within the pirate ranks; that article remained the same as in the original. "Three: First time offenders are to be whipped, then released. Repeated offenses will result in death. Four: For deserting or going AWOL, a man's ears will be sliced off and he will be paraded through his squadron for everyone to see." Ching glared at Zhu like he had cited rules that were designed specifically for him. A man of Zhu's integrity could not bear to lose face in front of his peers.

"And number five," Madam Choi said. "If a pirate rapes a woman, he will be put to death. If sex is consensual, the man will be beheaded and the woman cast overboard with a weight attached to her legs." Madam Choi turned her stern glare to Ching. "Finally, women captives are to be released. The most beautiful may be kept for wives and concubines, and the ugliest returned to shore. The rest are to be ransomed. Pirate men must be faithful to their wives. Are we agreed?"

Ching nodded, and rose. "Now, I go to choose my wife."

%%%

Madam Choi called the pirate captains to meet at the opium den on shore. She arrived dressed in the garb of a supreme pirate chief. On her silk tunic was a tapestry of dragons in azure, purple and red, accented with bits of jade and ivory stitched with braided silver-gold thread. Li had seen this uniform once before, when she accidentally found it among Madam Choi's things, and she had wondered then why the impoverished sea gypsy had not sold the splendid garment to feed her family. Now she understood: Madam Choi's entrance was an unmistakable message to the pirates present.

The costume was her late husband's official uniform, a uniform the pirate widow had dared not wear until she was certain of her leadership. On her head was Choi's war helmet and in her sash were his swords. Each member of each squadron sliced his finger and vowed to keep to the code, and as the blood spilled from the voluntary wounds, every drop was collected and stoppered in a ceramic jar. The half-filled jar of blood was kept with the code in Madam Choi's cabin.

Li was put in charge of piloting the ferryboat. She had spent half her life pretending to be a boy — so masquerading as the incompetent skipper of a ferryboat was easy.

The *Say Leng* was making her return journey tonight. Madam Choi organized a fleet of five hundred to assail her. The pirates knew that the merchant junk had two hundred men aboard her; they were taking no chances. Madam Choi left Number's Four and Five Daughters to babysit Wu.

"Stay away from Esen," Li ordered her son as she prepared for the mission. "Do not, under any circumstances, go near him."

Li donned her garb of ferryboat skipper and took her boat between the shore and the outer islands, and this time there was no green paint and white fuzzy bamboo flowers. No rat's blood. Zhu joined as her first mate, and the passengers of the ferryboat were made up of five pirates in peasant disguises.

The merchant junk was following the coastline. Li knew they would be on the lookout for pirates; she must move slow and carefully, so as not to risk her crew's lives.

"What are you doing?" Zhu demanded, when he saw that they were going offcourse. "Where did you learn to handle a ferryboat or any boat at all?" He paused for a breath, realized the folly of her intentions. "From Madam Choi? It's a wonder that woman hasn't killed all of us already."

"If you're going to hinder me Zhu, go below," Li said. "Better yet, make yourself useful."

Zhu slapped a meaty hand on hers, threatening to take the helm. "What's your plan? If it is what I think it is, it's a bad plan."

Li ripped her fingers out from under his and glared at him. "Why did you bother to stay? Why did you promise Madam Choi that you would serve her if you're only going to get in the way? Now move. I have work to do."

"I promised Quan that when I found you again, I would keep you safe. I fear I am failing."

Li was silent.

"He loves you still."

"Then where is he? Why send you in his place when he could come himself?" She followed his gaze to his right hand. "Where is your gemstone?"

"I left it on the junk for safekeeping."

"That was probably a good idea. The pirates keep eyeing it. It has great value. And they don't like you. In the heat of the raid, they would probably slice off your hand and not think twice about it." She paused as something occurred to her. "But the gemstone's value isn't monetary, is it, Zhu? Why do you and Madam Choi keep staring at it? Even Tao mentioned it."

"It has the power of seeing. But since I joined this pirate's brigade, it has closed its eye to me. I cannot see what battles Chi Quan is fighting, and what keeps him on the frontier."

Li glanced to the open sea. The scalp beneath her topknot prickled. She wanted to ask more about the gemstone, but now was not the time. "Stand down, Zhu. And brace yourself."

Her years of training with Master Yun and the work on the border walls had sharpened her reflexes; she threw the helm to the right and aimed the ferryboat into the reef. She ordered her crew to light lanterns and send the SOS signal just as the ferryboat scuttled in the channel. They hit rock, and water bled into the hull.

"Are you crazy?" Zhu shouted as they started to sink.

Moonlight blinked from behind a cloud, and movement among the lanterns aboard the merchant ship told her the *Say Leng*'s watchmen had sighted the scuttled ferryboat. The junk rocked against the tide, pressing staunchly toward them. Li sought the dagger in her boot and the sabre at her hip, before squinting beyond the black sea to where the others waited in the island coves.

%%%

Esen woke up to blackness. He heard the sound of female voices: captives, not the girl children of the junk. His throat hurt and his eyes were sticky. What had that little brat done to him? A four-year-old had stabbed him in the throat, incapacitating him instantly, and only because he had been unprepared. He scrutinized his dark prison. Where was he? From the sound of the water sloshing against the hull, he figured he was in the hold of the junk. Had the pirates gone on another raid? The thump of footfalls sounded overhead, and a small shadow appeared at the overhead grate. Someone squatted with a lantern and a child's face peered down at him. So, the little warrior had come to gloat.

Esen tried to speak, and choked from pain, swallowed, relaxed his throat muscles and crooked a finger, beckoning the boy closer.

"So, you are awake, barbarian," Wu said.

"I need water," Esen answered.

"Ma-ma says I am not to go near you."

"You don't have to come near me. Just get one of the girls to fetch me a drink." Wu's bright black eyes stared at him; then he rose.

When the water arrived, Wu dropped the water-filled bladder between the grate's iron bars. So much for trying to grab the little guy's hand and break his arm. For a teacup-sized imp, he was smart. And though he may be smart, he was little more than a baby.

A glint caused by the lantern light caught Esen's eye, and he saw that the boy was wearing a large gemstone, mounted on a gold band, looped to a thick string around his neck.

"What have you got there little one," he whispered, and reached out, tried to rise and Wu leaped back. "Give that gemstone to me. It is dangerous in the hands of a small boy."

Wu refused, covered the gemstone with his fingers and rubbed it back and forth. "It belongs to the warrior monk, He Zhu. You cannot have it!" As he spoke these words, he dropped the Tiger's Eye as though it burned. Unfortunately for Esen, it didn't fall far. It still dangled on the piece of string tied around the boy's neck. But the gemstone stirred. It's saffron brown colours moved and swirled, and suddenly an image grew out of the stone.

A young warrior in Mongol dress stood outside a felt tent, his falconer-gloved hand raised high. Esen could barely keep his eyes from forcing their way out of their sockets. Hundreds of thousands of horsemen hailed the great falconer before he turned to take the hand of a beautiful, black-haired woman in a snowy gown. Her feral eyes flashed above scarlet lips, and he recognized Jasmine. The warrior who had taken her hand as though he possessed her was none other than Altan.

The size of Wu's eyes rivaled Esen's own, so round were they with astonishment. He reached out to touch the vision, and Esen snatched at the gemstone through the grate of the hold, but the boy jerked out of reach. As he did so, the vision vanished.

"Bring it back! Bring back the vision. I must see what my baby brother is up to!"

Wu stared at Esen, dumbfounded, still dazed by what had happened.

"He Zhu will be angry with me," Wu said, clutching the gemstone in his babyish fist. "I must put it back." He ran as though a ghost was after him, no more than a terrified little boy.

Esen reached up. He must get that stone. Altan planned to usurp him did he? Jasmine had betrayed him, abandoned him. The prophecy was wrong: it was not the son of Lotus Lily that was a danger to him; it was his own brother.

Esen coughed, sputtered, pretended to be dying, and called to the girls above in a rasping, helpless voice. There was a reason he had been allowed to live, a reason why the pirate woman had healed his wound. They wanted him alive and so the girls who were left as his keepers were obligated to come to his aid.

"What do you want?" Number Four Daughter

demanded. "We gave you water. Why haven't you drunk it? I can see the water bladder on the floor by your feet."

"Help me," Esen said. "The air in here is unbreathable. I'm bleeding again. I will die."

Number Four Daughter tipped her lit lantern toward him, causing the yellow flame within to flicker. It was dark in the hold and he covered the wound with his hand to mask the bandage.

"Your mother, the captain of this junk, will be angry if you let me die."

"I can't come down there," she said. "None of us can lift the iron grate."

Esen rose unsteadily to his feet. He had to make this look good to convince the girl of his feebleness, and shoved a hand against the grate. It was too heavy for one man to lift from this angle and impossible for a child or even three.

"Call one of the captive women," he said. "I can hear their voices."

"They are bound hand and foot. They cannot come."

"Untie them."

The girl shook her head.

"Then I will die." For emphasis, Esen sank to a prostrate pose. With the lantern poised under her chin, the girl's features were distorted, and she looked worried.

The look soon vanished because the girl was almost as ruthless as her mother, even though she was only eight years old. "I guess that can't be helped."

She left, abandoning him to his prison. He rose again and peered into the night sky; the stars shivered. He heard the women talking again. They were not far from him. If only he had the full volume of his voice. He tried to shout. His voice came out gruff and painfully raspy. He rattled a silver ring he wore on his finger against the iron grate.

Finally, he heard a thump and a dragging sound. This continued for a few minutes, before a woman's head appeared over the grate. "Are you a prisoner like us?" she asked.

"Yes." He kept his face in shadow so that she couldn't see that he wasn't Chinese. "I can't speak loudly because those rogues have sliced my throat."

"The beasts," she said. "They're forcing me to marry one of their captains."

"You needn't suffer that fate. If you help me get out of here, I will rescue you all. How many are you?"

"Four women and two children. A girl and a boy."

Good enough, he thought. The strength of six people and himself should be able to lift this iron grate sufficiently for him to slide it aside. "Are your hands free?"

"No, but the children's are."

"Good. Tell them to find something to lever this grate with—a pole, a trident. Anything the pirates have left behind."

The captive children found a broken halberd and with that, and the help of the other women who managed to drag themselves to the hold and climb to their feet, they adequately pried the grate free so that Esen could use his brute strength and shove it away. He was amazed at what these women could do when spurred. Despite having their hands bound in front of them and their crippled feet shackled at the ankles, collectively they were able to generate sufficient leverage.

Esen leaped up and hoisted himself out of the hold, ignoring the pleas of the women who had rescued him and were now begging for him to untie them. Instead, he threatened them with the sharp, broken end of the halberd, and ordered them to squat on the deck; and then he tore the skirts of two of the women and used the strips of cloth to bind the children's hands and feet, before he shoved them down into the hold, followed by their protesting mothers. Afterward, he went in search of Wu and the Tiger's Eye.

%%%

The *Say Leng* hove to and stayed just outside the reef. A

watchman hailed them through a blow horn, and Li responded by requesting their help. All was quiet for a while, then activity started on the merchant junk: lanterns were lit and seamen prepared to toss grappling hooks to the ferryboat. When they saw that it was too badly damaged to be towed, they changed tactics and prepared to lower lifeboats instead.

"How many!" the captain of the *Say Leng* shouted.

"Thirty passengers," Li lied. "And five crew!"

She turned to He Zhu raised her dagger to his throat, and his eyes widened in surprise. "If you cannot be loyal to Madam Choi, then I will have to tie you up." She loosened the sash from her waist to show that she meant every word she said.

He grabbed her wrist and would have shaken the blade from her hand, had she not tripped him onto the floor, her foot swinging out from under him before she stomped it onto his chest.

"You have learned much of fighting since I saw you last," Zhu gasped.

Li grasped the dagger firmly in her fist, her foot pressing near his throat. "Working on the wall at the frontier was a good teacher. Swear, Zhu, on the life of Chi Quan's son, that you will not betray Madam Choi."

He swallowed, his voice cracking. "I swore it once to her. And I swear again to you. I will not betray her."

She hesitated, removed her foot from his chest and extended her hand. He took it and pulled himself up. Li shot him one last look and went to the rail while Zhu followed, slapping salt and grime from his tunic.

A number of serpent boats were gliding over the waves toward the merchant junk, and the captain of the *Say Leng*, too busy sending a rescue mission to the scuttled ferryboat, failed to see them.

A soft sloshing sound came from the side of the ferryboat, and Li moved to the rail and looked down. At first she saw nothing, only darkness. Then a man scaled the hull to the top and scanned the deck, a strange, puzzled expression on his face. "Where are all your passengers?"

Before he could blink, Li drew her dagger on him and ordered him aboard. One other rowboat followed, and under knifepoint, she ordered that sailor to board as well. Across the reef, the merchant junk was flooded with pirates armed with tridents and sabres, and Li turned to He Zhu. "Tie up these men."

"The ferryboat is sinking!" he objected.

Yes, the deck was slowly taking on water. *So let it sink.* Zhu glowered an accusation. Had she become a murderer as well as a pirate? No. The wild-eyed look of the two captured merchant sailors changed her mind. "All right then," she said. "They come with us. But bind their hands."

%%%

Where was the little Chinese brat? He must find that gemstone. It had powers beyond his most ambitious dreams. Even Jasmine did not own a jewel such as this.

Esen crept to the hatch where he could hear the sighs of sleeping children. If any of these pirate spawn gave him trouble he would show no mercy. He looked to the floor where three bundles lay, and the moonlight painted their faces with silver — while the eyes of one glinted. He slapped a hand over the boy's mouth, and whispered, "If you wake the girls, I will kill them with my bare hands." He slowly removed his hand from Wu's lips, which were trembling. "Get out of your bed and come with me."

Wu left his tatty sleeping furs, and followed out of the hatchway and onto the moonlit deck. Esen quietly shut the hatch, and when he reached the ship's hold he stopped. The captive women that had rescued him were cowering at the bottom, eyes bright with fear, the grate casting crisscross shadows on their faces — securely trapped. He squatted so that he was at the level of the little boy. "Give me the gemstone."

"I don't have it. I returned it to Lieutenant He Zhu's mantle where I found it."

He grabbed Wu's wrist, and the little boy squeaked. "Show me," Esen rasped.

The gemstone lay inside a hidden pocket of Lieutenant He Zhu's mantle, which was folded under a bench inside Madam Choi's cabin. The golden band on which the stone was set was looped to a strong piece of string. Esen scooped up the gemstone and took it outside. He had almost forgotten about the boy until he saw him, out of the corner of his eye, run to the hatchway where the pirate girls slept. Two flying leaps with his stout legs brought him to the hatch, and he looped the string with the gemstone over his head and hoisted Wu by the collar. "Oh, no you don't. I still owe you for this!" He jabbed a thumb at his bandaged throat.

Esen tore a strip of cloth from the boy's ratty shirt and tied his hands together in front of him. From now until they reached the Forbidden City, the brat would be his constant companion.

It was two hours before dawn. They must get off this boat. It was anchored in a cove, not far from shore. How long had he been unconscious, drugged by the pirate witchdoctor? Certainly, they were no longer in the land of the dead bamboo. He shaded his eyes to judge the distance to shore, searched the sky, and then lowered his gaze. The landscape was familiar: a tree-lined escarpment overlooked the shallow beach. He tucked the boy under his arm and dropped down into one of the rafts that were fastened to the junk. He released the rope and poled the raft away.

Negotiating the black sea by sight alone hurt his eyes, and he squeezed back the burning tears, tasting the salt on his lips. The air was raw. Breathing the biting wind cut into his injured throat like a sharp knife, and he swallowed with renewed pain. On the far shore, he recognized the jungle, and somewhere among the trees was the path that led to the lagoon. Could the magic that had occurred there happen again?

He dragged the raft to shore and hauled the boy under his arm, stunned that the little mite had cost him his voice. He could whisper quite loud, but not shout. Maybe that was just as well; silence might be his best friend under the circumstances.

Moonlight struck some white berries on shrubbery banking the jungle, the same fruit he had consumed the last time he was here. They grew thick and bubbly on clustered branches. He had been starving and had eaten them without knowing what they were then, and so again, he grabbed a handful with his free hand, before guessing his way along the path to the lagoon.

The moon was bright enough to bring white light into the glade. All was as it was before when he learned to tame the *Fenghuang*.

On a rock overlooking the blue-green pool stood a crane, its smooth white neck shining like satin, and below it, a wall of stones showed sharp and deep. In the center, the water was dark, and shadows moved as the trees above shifted in the breeze. A mist hovered lightly over the surface and moonbeams penetrated the mist, reflecting a pale spectrum of colours.

The boy wriggled under his arm. "Be still," he ordered.

He dropped the boy on his bottom, the mist parted and he waited. The crane was gone. A giant bird with the head of a golden pheasant, the tail of an azure peacock and the legs of a crane, took its place. Wu screamed, went silent when Esen kicked him. Even the boy recognized the creature haloed by the bold face of the moon: *Fenghuang*, the shape-shifting Chinese Phoenix that one saw only on painted vases and tapestries, and heard about from faerie stories. Its long graceful wings spread wide and it came toward Esen. This time he was ready.

"Why does it not kill you?" Wu asked. "The phoenix is

a symbol of high virtue and grace. It is a symbol of power sent from the heavens to the empress." He paused for a moment. "That would be my mother—"

"I told you to shut your trap."

"*Fenghuang* will only stay if the ruler is without darkness and corruption."

"For a boy, little more than a baby, you know too much."

"I will be a great warrior like my father."

Esen shot Wu a wilting look. "You also talk too much."

He approached the phoenix, one fist clutched toward it. While the berries had done nothing adverse to him, they seemed to have a strange hallucinatory effect on the phoenix, putting it in a state of rapture that made it obey him. He had fashioned a necklet of the berries, which he had strung around its enormous neck, and it hung there still, the tiny fruits dried to wrinkled pearls.

He fed the giant bird new berries from his cupped hand, and immediately, it grew complacent and bathed in the lagoon. He strung what remained with a vine and looped the fresh necklet over the phoenix's head, then grappled Wu by the arm and said, "We're going for a ride."

CHAPTER SEVEN
The Demise of the *Say Leng*

Bound and gagged, all that was visible of the captured soldiers in the dark sea night was the pallor of their faces as they were herded into the rowboats they had arrived in. When Li's crew were also safely aboard, she abandoned the ferryboat to its fate and turned her attention to the cries of astonishment as the *Say Leng's* officers realized they'd been duped.

The merchant junk was close enough now so that Li could watch the battle on her decks. Men ran helter-skelter. The explosive sound of a blunderbuss sent a palpable backdraft across the water. The *Say Leng's* men had firearms, but it was too late for them to use their cannons. They were already boarded. And they were no match for the blades and pikes of the pirates. Cargo junks were notoriously ill armed, and they had a miscellany of old matchlocks and bird guns. Chinese muskets were wretched things, crudely made and of small calibre, with large touchholes. If the charge did not blow out the back, it often escaped forward, because the ball was inserted without wad or ramming.

Li took in a breath, glanced back at Zhu who was rowing, and braced herself. They had been sighted. From where she sat at the head of one of the rowboats, she had a clear view of a sailor attempting to light a slow-burning cord over the hole with which to fire a decrepit matchlock at them. She did not waver. By her orders, the two commandeered rowboats steadfastly retained their heading, and only stopped at her signal, when they were just short of colliding with the junk's hull. Li tossed a grappling hook overhead to the deck and raised her pike, a deadly sharp, sabre-like blade, now aimed at her would-be sniper, while her small crew brandished a medley of short pikes sharpened at either end, a woodcutter's billhook and long-handled knives with iron-tipped blades that served as swords. As the sailor with the long-burning wick tilted his matchlock, Li raised her tightly woven rattan shield, but the wick fizzled out before the poor soul could fire a shot, and the man fled.

In the chaos, she tried to find Madam Choi, sighted her on the quarterdeck fighting hand-to-hand combat with one of the junk's officers, her sabre flashing and her colourful silk tunic glimmering in the lantern light. The *Say Leng* had too many sailors, and Li hollered up to her captain that they should retreat. "No!" the pirate woman shouted between slashes of her sword. "Not until Number One Daughter is avenged!"

A ball of fire came flying out of the dark and landed nearby, and Li turned and saw Ching's fleet. He and his pirates were hurling firebrands at the sails from out of long hollow bamboo stalks. Li gasped as she realized the viciousness of his plan; from his flagship, 'stinkpots' flew at the enemy. The earthenware pots were filled with gunpowder and liquor, and pieces of ignited charcoal were put into their lids and the pots suspended from the masthead in bags. The pirates were aiming the stinkpots straight at the *Say Leng*'s decks.

She dived at Zhu and he lost his footing as she dragged him down, a stinkpot shattering, and igniting the gunpowder and sending up fire and smoke, and a horrific smell. Several of the merchant seamen lay dead or wounded by the blast, and the planks were ablaze. Ching had lost his mind and they had to get off this ship.

Li looked to Madam Choi. She had witnessed the blast after incapacitating her opponent, and now swung down the halyard to join her companions, who had risen to their feet.

"This attack with stinkpots wasn't sanctioned," Li said.

"Irrelevant now," Madam Choi answered. "The *Say Leng* is doomed and all of her men with her. They can't put out the fire."

Li grabbed her captain's arm, catching her tunic sleeve at the same time, and then let go as she suffered the ferocity of the pirate woman's glare. She bowed apologetically for daring to touch the official costume of the Chief of Pirates. "We leave then?" she asked humbly.

"Not until I kill the man who murdered my child."

"He'll die anyway," Li said. "The flames will see to that."

"*I* have to see it."

"How will you find him in this bedlam?"

The dark eyes moved ever so slightly, a thin crescent of white showing at the bottom of her black irises. "I see him now."

She sheathed her sabre and lifted a trident that was lying on the deck, stalked through the blaze, insensible to the grasping fires that exploded all around her, and deliberately and single-mindedly forced her way toward the sailor who had taken her daughter's life. He recognized her, saw the demonic rage on her face and raced to the bow, but Madam Choi was directly behind him and aimed her trident at his back, hurled it as though she were harpooning a whale, sending him screaming as the three-pronged weapon speared him between the shoulder blades, toppling him into the sea.

Li squeezed her eyelids tight, the heat of the flames baking her, eyeballs burning and tearing from the incessant smoke. She felt Zhu's hand on her shoulder. "It's over," he said. "She can't expect more from us. Let's go. Wu is waiting."

She inhaled. That was a mistake, coughed—the acrid air choking her—and rubbed smoke from her eyes. Sailors were racing in a panic, some throwing themselves off the ship rather than standing about helplessly, waiting to be consumed by the flames. A few stalwart souls tried to put out the fires with heavy blankets. It was pointless.

Many of Ching's pirates had looted the ship while Madam Choi and the others were fighting. Now the thieves were tossing goods and silver to the serpent boats below. Out on the water—safely out of harm's way on his pirate junk—Captain Ching orchestrated the retreat of his rogues.

Re-joining her associate, Madam Choi barely acknowledged the hand he extended to haul her aboard his junk. She turned to the merchant ship floundering in the sea, and saw that the large husk no longer resembled a sea-going vessel. With her bamboo sails incinerated and the booms long fallen, the ship cracked and broke like a fortune cookie left too long in the oven. She watched it writhe and burn to smoldering timbers as they weighed anchor and made sail with every pirate accounted for.

When they reached the cove where Madam Choi's junk sat anchored, Ching was invited aboard to discuss division of the loot and the ransom of captives. As soon as he boarded, Madam Choi lit into him. "Do you realize what you've done? Now the Imperial Navy will have no choice but to rout us out!"

Ching snorted. "She was a prize."

"What kind of prize is it that you burn!"

"Those sailors were in the way. The captain refused to hand over the ship."

"How do you know? You were not aboard the *Say Leng!*"

He sneered. "You are the Chief of Pirates." He bowed, but by the tone of his voice, Li knew he was mocking Madam Choi. "There is room for only one leader on a raid. You had not convinced the *Say Leng's* captain to release her. I saw the chaos. You had a mind for one thing and one thing only. Revenge. While revenge is well and good, those who aid you in your vendetta must be paid. I took steps to ensure there would be payment." He nodded at the serpent boats loaded with booty and the captive sailors who had tried to escape a fiery death only to end up prisoners of the ruthless

Ching. "Those captured include the ship's officers. They will bring in a pretty sum. That, plus the ransom we get for the women you took from the ferryboat will pay my men for their troubles."

His men? Li exchanged looks with Zhu. Madam Choi's face was streaked with sweat and grime, but that did not mask her fury. A trickle of blood leaked from a flesh wound beneath her right temple. "Even as we speak, the word is out concerning the burning of the *Say Leng* and the massacre of its crew. The White Tiger seeks us."

Ching screwed up his nose, the flaring nostrils snorting like an ox. "The White Tiger is a myth. The actual man who stands in his shoes is a poor excuse for a Sea Dog. He is all puff and no bite. Under His Most Honourable Supreme Chief Choi, our past leader and your late husband, the Imperial Navy failed to stop us—and it will not stop us now."

Li had had enough for one night. She left the bickering pirate captains and went to the hatch where the children slept, but when she opened the hatch, her heart stopped.

%%%

The girls were cowering in the shadows with fear distorting their features, and the only thing that showed up clearly was the ring of white around their black eyes. They crawled nervously out of their hiding place while Li glanced frantically around. Wu was gone!

He Zhu reached out to stop her from unleashing her fear on the hapless youngsters who admitted to Wu's abduction by Esen. "They are only children, Li," he said, using a quiet voice.

"They are pirates. They know better. Wu is only four years old. They are older. They know not to trust a Mongol."

Madam Choi struck out a hand to stop the arguing. "Enough. She is right. The girls were left in charge. They were negligent. They will be punished."

"Come," Zhu said. "We shall question the captives.

Perhaps they can give us a lead as to what happened and where the barbarian has gone with Wu."

"What happened!" Li demanded of the female hostage when they had freed her from her prison. "How is it that you and the other captives are in the hold and the warlord is not!"

The woman shivered, refused to speak, knowing that anything she said would be used against her, and Madam Choi threatened to cane her, to string her up on the yardarm and flog her, but Ching stepped in and told them that the females would be worthless if they were marked.

"Esen could not have escaped without help," Madam Choi said.

Li interrupted, her nerves and her fear for her son overriding the fact that she was stepping out of line by cutting off the pirate chief's speech. "Madam," she said, addressing the prisoner respectfully. "No one will harm you. I don't care how the Mongol escaped. I only want to know where he has gone."

Tears streamed down the captive's cheeks and she no longer looked pretty. "I don't know where he has gone. I only know that he took the little boy and he took some kind of gemstone."

Zhu grabbed the woman by the shoulders, and Ching seized Zhu by the wrist and forced him to release her. "I won't hurt you," Zhu said. "You say the Mongol took some kind of gemstone with him? How do you know that if you couldn't see? You said that you and the others were tossed below into the hold."

"I heard the beast talking. The two of them, the barbarian and the boy were standing over the grate, and I overheard him ask the boy to take him to the gemstone."

"What does this mean?" Li asked Zhu. "How would Wu know about your gemstone?"

"He saw it on my finger. And you know how little boys are. They are like parrots and monkeys, fascinated by shiny objects. He must have watched me hide it before we left for the raid."

"But why would Esen want the gemstone? On the surface it is only a bauble and not a terribly fine one at that. It is saffron brown, nothing very special in colour."

Madam Choi scowled, nodded. "Your concern is not unfounded, Li. He could have taken the trinkets we stole from these captives. Their possessions combined—silver bracelets and gold rings—are of more obvious value than a plain brown stone. In fact, the ransom he could have gotten from these women would have far exceeded anything he could get from the gemstone—unless he knew its true worth."

He Zhu's brow furrowed, and Ching turned his hands palms up. "What is all this fuss about a plain brown stone? What is it worth? I thought you wanted your son back," he said to Li.

She was not going to say anymore in the presence of the despicable pirate, and from the narrowed eyes of Madam Choi it was clear she agreed, and He Zhu had ceased speaking the moment he realized Ching was interested in his gemstone.

"It is nothing, only a family heirloom belonging to the warrior monk," Madam Choi said. "Li, take one of the serpent boats and go ashore. Find out what you can of Esen's trail. He couldn't have gone far. The closest land is that escarpment there, overlooking the jungle. Zhu, you go with her. Ching and I will settle business. Then I will join you in the search for your son."

They unfastened a serpent boat from the side of the junk and rowed shoreward. Zhu was a strong oarsman and they hit land in twenty minutes. They beached the serpent boat on the sand and followed a track of footprints that led toward the jungle.

"There is only one set of prints," Zhu said.

"Naturally," Li answered. "The barbarian would have

been carrying Wu. Can you imagine Wu going willingly?"

This drew a brief smile from Zhu. The boy had stabbed his captor once before when he was taken against his will, and Li only hoped that her son would not try something so foolhardy again without his mother to protect him.

They followed the path through the jungle. Esen was not concerned about leaving a trail, and this made Li suspicious. Why would the Mongol wish them to follow him so easily?

They entered the clearing and her mind swarmed with memories. She squashed them as though she were flattening a fly.

The lagoon was as she remembered, except this time there was no crane standing at the far side of the pool, and the surrounding shrubbery was thick with white berries — but otherwise the scene was the same.

"What a beautiful pool," Zhu said, and glanced swiftly at Li. No doubt he remembered looking down from the cliff top and seeing her and his captain in the water. "Something was dropped here. There are scuffle marks. I think the boy was put on the ground."

The prints moved to the edge of the lagoon, then ended. Had they gone into the water? But if they had, where did they go from there?

He Zhu crouched, lifted something from the bank, and pinched a gold and azure feather between his fingertips. "It's the same kind of feather that Tao found near Esen on board the pirate junk."

Fenghuang. The Chinese Phoenix. What did it mean? Wherever the warlord went, a feather was left.

"This is not helping," she said, frustrated, tears threatening to spill. "We are not getting any closer to finding Wu. He can't just have disappeared."

"He did not disappear. Esen has him. And I believe he is safe."

"How can he be safe as long as he is in the hands of that

savage. Esen wants him dead. He wants *me* dead. But if he can't have me, he will settle for Wu."

Zhu's face looked puzzled as he raised his eyes to meet hers. "I no longer think he wants Wu dead."

"What do you mean? All he has wanted, since the day you and Quan brought him to the Forbidden City to be dined by the Emperor, was to see Wu dead. He never wanted him to be conceived, no less born."

"No more," Zhu said, shaking his head. "Esen has learned of the gemstone's power. I am sure of it."

Li's eyes widened until she was certain her lids would split from the force. "But he can't use it. Only one with the gift can open the Tiger's Eye. What can the gemstone possibly have to do with Wu?"

Zhu searched the dark water in the center of the pool and the turquoise shallows, and Li strained her eyes to follow. The mist sparkled with the sun's rays; tiny lights flittered among the mist, then dispersed. Oh, if only Wu knew how to summon the Ghostfire. It would have protected him, shielded him from the barbarian's eyes. Maybe that was what had happened. Had Wu discovered the magic of *Gwei-huo*? Had he deceived the Mongol warlord and escaped? And even now, could he be hiding somewhere nearby in the jungle?

"Zhu," she said. "I think maybe Wu is not far from here."

Zhu fingered the feather in his hand and shook his head in full disagreement. "He is long gone."

"No. I can summon the power of *Gwei-huo*. If I can do that, maybe my son can, too."

"That is not his power."

"How do you know? I am his mother. If I have this power, then why shouldn't he have it? If he does, maybe when Esen's attention was drawn elsewhere he found a chance to run and hide."

"Perhaps. But if he is hiding, why doesn't he show

himself? He isn't deaf. We haven't lowered our voices. We have been standing here for many minutes, nattering loud enough for the fish to hear. It is only us looking for him. And you are his mother."

True. If Wu was anywhere within earshot, he would have shown himself by now. Li wiped her wet cheek with the back of her hand. No time for tears. Weakness would not help her to find her son.

"I think it is as Tao suspects," Zhu said. "Esen has found a way to tame *Fenghuang*. She is his transport. And he has taken Wu with him."

"But where have they gone?"

"If I am right about the gemstone, Esen has taken Wu and the ring to the Forbidden City. Now he has something to barter with."

"The Emperor will not believe that Wu is his grandson. Not without proof. And if Jasmine has re-joined His Majesty, his life won't be worth a grain of rice."

"Oh, but you're wrong, Li. Your boy is now worth much more to Esen alive than he is worth to him dead. You see... the gemstone speaks to Wu—just as it speaks to me."

"How can that be?" She narrowed her eyes suspiciously but she wasn't sure of what she suspected.

"There are many questions yet to be answered," he said. "I don't know why the gemstone speaks to your son or why it speaks to me. It would not speak for Master Yun. But that is the only reason I can think of why Esen would have taken the boy alive."

"Then we must locate Master Yun and learn why the gemstone has chosen my son. But first we must *find* my son."

"My thoughts exactly. We inform Madam Choi of our plan, then we ride." He spun on his heel and forged through the jungle path back to the beach where the serpent boat waited for them. Li helped Zhu haul the boat onto the water, but just as the waves caught the keel, Zhu sucked in a gasp.

"What is it?" She turned to look in the direction that he was squinting.

Out on the milky horizon, against the bright morning pallor, a ship moved toward the consortium of pirate boats anchored in the outer bay. The ship was behind an island at the cove's entrance, and would not be visible to the trio of pirate vessels. But it was in full sail, and it was only a matter of time before the pirates would be exposed. Li clenched her fists, knuckles whitening.

Zhu released the bow of the serpent boat, and lifted a small spyglass that was hooked to his sash while Li struggled to hold the boat from escaping.

"Imperial colours. The hunt is on."

"We must warn them," she said.

"I can't go with you. I am a fugitive. My face is known, and only my helmet hides my identity. I will go after the warlord and Wu by land. You return to Madam Choi quickly, and warn her of the impending danger."

A childish impulse overwhelmed her. "I want to go with you." She released the serpent boat, but grabbed at it at the last minute before the backwash swept it away.

"Your choice," he said, and tucked his spyglass into his sash. "I have a horse. She is somewhere in the jungle foraging." He whistled a high-pitched tune and was answered with a whinny. "She hears me and harkens. Come. We have no time to waste."

"Wait." Li turned wet eyes to Zhu. "I cannot leave without warning Madam Choi. But I don't want you to waste time coming with me. Go and find the barbarian who abducted my son. Kill him. I will follow shortly."

"You have no horse, Li. You can't get far by foot."

"I am hoping I won't have to. Madam Choi's pirate junk is swift. She will take me north to the Yellow Sea. We'll travel up the Grand Canal to Beijing. From there I will find my way to the Forbidden City."

"Xiang Gong protect you," he said.

"And may Lei Shen protect *you*."

Zhu's mount burst through the trees and stopped in front of her rider. He leaped upon the sleek mare's back and caught the reins, while Li climbed aboard the serpent boat and aimed it in the direction of the unsuspecting pirates.

CHAPTER EIGHT
The White Tiger

Admiral Lao Hu Fong had heard about the pirates headed by a woman. In the Waterworld, women were full participants in life at sea. It was so different from the world he came from where women worked at home. This woman was an aberration, a bad influence. Some reports even painted her as a cannibalistic monster, and those lucky enough to escape her raids told tales of cruel and inhuman punishment. She was an exhibitionist, they said, a ruthless and bestial captor. One instance told of a captive being fixed upright against the mainmast, his bowels sliced open, and his heart scooped out. The heart, still pumping, was soaked in rice spirits, then fried and eaten by the pirate chief herself. At last report, she had stolen a ferryboat by subversive means, looted and burned a merchant junk, and taken captives from both. He hated to think what she had done with these.

There were reports, too, of one of her lieutenants, deemed choicest of all the females in the pirate squads. She was taller than her compatriots, gloriously formed, and when confronted by the beauty of her face, the thoughts of men went stupid.

He was keen to meet this lieutenant; she might make him a good wife.

Admiral Fong signaled to his helmsman to bring the vessel to, slacken sails and ride slowly and with ease. The pirates had not sighted him yet while the island stood between them. But the watch had spied a single serpent boat heading for the pirate junks, and through his spyglass, its pilot looked slight but highly skilled. Long, black hair flowed from beneath a loosened topknot that threatened to unravel completely in the wind, and the sea splashed wildly over the gunwales of the slender boat, soaking its rower. The loose shirt on the labouring figure wrestled the wind and it was soon apparent that this was no man, but a girl.

"Heave to and take the serpent boat and her pilot," he ordered his captain. The captain repeated the order down the line. The girl noticed their change of course and started waving her arms at the pirate flagship.

"Bear down," Fong ordered, and turned to study the long shadow of the junk that stretched beyond the island. "No. Belay that. Hold her steady. Take a tender and bring the serpent boat and her occupant aboard."

The girl was now standing, signaling desperately, and orders were dispatched for more boats to surround the three pirate vessels. The serpent boat was hailed, but its occupant merely hoisted a sabre to warn the Emperor's navy from trying to seize her. One of the seamen hooked the lip of her boat, yanked hard, toppling her into the water, and then dived in as she floundered to the surface, coughing and spitting, encumbered by her clothing. She had dropped her weapon in the fall and, for a moment, Fong lost sight of her in a shimmering fog.

She might have escaped if the sailor wasn't already gripping her securely, befuddled though he was. Despite her thrashing he was stronger, and because he held tight even as her flailing sent the luminescence flying, he managed to haul her up and away to where his mate leaned forward in their rowboat.

They roughly laced her wrists and ankles with ropes, trussing her like an ewe, and when they re-joined the warship, they passed her hand over foot to the waiting men on deck. Fong hollered down that she should be brought to him in his quarters after she was properly dried and dressed. Fong was not ignorant of the needs of women. On occasion he had brought ladies aboard and laden them with generous gifts, but he never kept them long, and had made none his wife. So far, no one was worthy of the position.

Her hair was ink-black, now combed out and full. Her dark eyes were sharp. Coral pins gleamed in her silky tresses, and the earrings and bracelets he had ordered her adorned in were of the same delicate melon-pink stone. She was superbly displayed in white satin decorated with pink pearl buttons, and on her feet were white silk slippers.

Fong signaled her escort to untie her hands so that she might kneel before him. Her feet were not deformed as Chinese custom prescribed, and the moment her hands were free, she sprang at him. He laughed.

"Do you promise to behave yourself if I don't have your hands and feet bound?"

Plainly, she was ready to claw out his eyes, but she nodded and dropped her hands to her side.

Smart girl.

She was probably barely twenty. Every motion she made spoke of contempt, but he signed for the guards to leave them alone. "I see you have accepted my gifts and my hospitality," Fong said, strutting toward her.

"Only because I did not wish to remain in those sodden clothes."

"I thought you'd be unable to resist. After all, you *are* a pirate. You are indeed a great beauty; the stories told of you are true. What is your name? You might as well tell me. I will get it out of you eventually. After I take the ships of your chief, Madam Choi."

"Leave them alone," she said.

Admiral Fong lowered his eyes to the hollow of her throat where a circlet of jade—not one of his pieces—was nestled. He lifted it from her suntanned skin, frowning as he recognized the insignia impressed on the clasp of the solid gold chain. "This belongs to the Imperial house. What are you doing with it?"

She snatched it from his fingers, nearly breaking it. His brow knit until he felt even the furrows on his forehead pucker, and he inspected her more closely, for he had heard stories of the escaped princess. Could this be her? "What is your name?"

This time it was not a question, but a command, and she smiled like she knew his suspicions. "If I tell you my name, if I am who you think I am, will you let my friends go?"

"Why should I do that? You are my prisoner and soon they will be, too." He touched a strand of her hair. "Tell me what happened out there. What was that mist that enshrouded you in luminescence?"

She yanked her head away. "Have you never seen the Ghostfire?"

"I have heard of it, though I've never seen it on the high seas. However, lately, there have been stories of hopping corpses and Will-o'-the-wisp." He paused. "So, these things are real. Why, then, did you not escape when you could? My men were blinded. You were invisible."

"Are you stupid, sir? I would have drowned."

Fong slapped her in the face and she recoiled. She rubbed her reddening cheek, scowled. Again she looked like she would gouge out his eyes, but she refrained. "My boat capsized and is now at the bottom of the sea. If you were watching, then you must have seen that."

"You are Lotus Lily," Admiral Fong said, decisively.

"I am and I am not." The girl spoke in an annoyingly ambiguous tone. "I prefer to be called Li."

He glowered. "Li is a man's name."

She shrugged. "As far as the water people are concerned, gender is unimportant—except when it comes to making children."

%%%

Admiral Fong was not an ugly man, but neither was he pretty. Compared to Chi Quan, whose magnificence was incomparable, this admiral—for she knew he was an admiral by the tunic and coat that he wore—this admiral's power came not from his actions but from his birth. He was one of those born into privilege, of a military family. She could tell by the cut of his chin and the straightness of his nose. No doubt his father was also an admiral. And his power came from his arrogance. While Quan was a man of courage and action, this officer seduced others to do his will lest he beat them.

"Now that you know my name, sir, I demand to know who it is that has detained me against my will." Li tossed her head like a tigress and planted her slim hands on her white-satin-covered hips.

The admiral pursed his lips, eyes glimmering with suppressed laughter. Would he strike her again if she persisted in her insolence? If he did, she would take it like a man.

His face suddenly went hard. "My name is Admiral Lao Hu Fong. And you will drop to your knees before me."

"You are not the Emperor. I drop to my knees for no one. Not even for him."

His hand snatched at a whip that was hanging on the bulkhead. "Obey me!"

Her cheek still stung from where he had struck her with his hand, and the whip's sting would feel like a knife after that. Li spread her skirt and lowered herself demurely to one knee. "What is your will, master?" she asked prissily, her sarcasm meant to slice deep.

His whip hand moved. Li raised her eyes and lashed out. "You dress me in this finery only to split it to rags?"

The whip snapped and landed on her shoulder, the tail scoring her cheek, sending agony from her shoulder to her face and down her arm. Blood seeped through the satin sleeve where the robe was splayed. Her lip trembled, and she bit it.

"Do not talk back to me again. Next time I will not flog you, I will rape you instead."

Tears streamed down Li's cheeks, mingling salt with blood. A pink stain bloomed on the front of the white satin robe as teardrops splashed onto her chest. "You think, to me, rape is a punishment?" She rose, no longer pretending to be afraid of him, and now not even conscious of the pain. "You can do nothing to me more torturous than detaining me from the search for my son." That seemed to stymie him for a second and Li took advantage of his indecision. "You know who I am," she said, sucking forth her courage. "Then you should know that the boy I seek is His Majesty's grandson."

His eyes dropped to the jade circlet, and he lifted it by its gold chain. "This is a royal stamp on the clasp."

"And you dare flog a princess of the Imperial Court?"

"You will fetch a pretty sum. His Majesty has placed a generous bounty on your head. He means to have you executed. As far as I am aware, there is no stipulation as to the condition of your body when I return it to him."

Li's heart fluttered. Fear was the same as excitement and excitement ruled fear.

And anger.

"Do not dare to defy me, girl. As you have tasted the sting of my lash first hand, you know that I have no problem using it." His eyes jerked to his whip hand, then down to the bloodied laceration on her shoulder. "Even on a damsel, such as you, with your tender flesh," he finished with mock softness.

"My flesh is no more tender than a goat's. Five years, eleven months and five days I have spent among the water people. We are a tough breed." She sucked on her lip when he did not answer, tasting dried tears. Her voice changed from hot to cold, and she wasted no words in accusing him. "You mean to return me to my father."

His eyes moved up and down, taking in every feature of her face and body, every curve of flesh and fold of satin. To him, she was still extraordinary despite the damage he had caused. "I have been looking for a wife, a woman of legendary beauty. With the mettle of a stormy sea."

"Let me get this straight," Li said. "You won't return me

to the Emperor for execution if I agree to marry you?"

Admiral Fong wet his lips. His dark eyes smiled, but his mouth did not.

"Do you know who I am?" he asked.

Yes, you just told me, she almost said, the scorn returning to her expression. She hiked her nose up into a wrinkle as deep as her memory of the Transcendent Pig's. Something stopped her from voicing her thoughts, and she lowered her eyes to the insignia tattooed on the back of his hand: a white tiger.

She gasped, and looked up to see his gaze burrowing into hers. If *she* was legendary, *he* was myth come alive.

"So, I am not a total stranger to you. At least, you have seen this before." He turned his hand, backside to her, and held it in front of her face.

It wasn't only the memory of Chao that she had brought back as a souvenir from her visit to the Etherworld. The black tattoo on the back of his hand reminded her of the beautiful garden with its origami-like flowers and fresh green grass. It also brought to mind the garden stone, the Taijitu carved on its surface and the strange words of Master Tong: *Come autumn, the White Tiger awaits you in the west.*

Was Admiral Lao Hu Fong this White Tiger? And what about the symbols on the Taijitu: the White Tigress and the Jade Dragon before they had transformed to the backward S of black and white? Was the White Tigress a premonition of things to come? Was he giving her a choice?

The last time she had chosen life. This time she would again choose life—but at what price? The White Tigress meant something. The White Tiger's mate was the wife of Admiral Fong. To choose otherwise would mean death. The Jade Dragon was the symbol of the Emperor—and the Emperor wanted her dead.

Li raised her eyes to the admiral, fell to her knees, and extended her fingers to his tattooed hand, which he gave. She held it in her palm like it was something precious. The tiger's head was half turned to her, its shoulders low and slouched. The thin black stripes interspersed with broad patches of white were unmistakably the markings of *Lao Hu*. His name was Lao Hu Fong. How could she have missed the obvious? She could only ascribe it to worry over her darling Wu and his godmother, Madam Choi. Li controlled her breathing. Her mockery of him was shielded from his spying eyes by her lowered lashes, but now she must gather all of her strength and do the best thing for all involved.

"I accept," she said, lifting her long, straight lashes at him, and returned his smile. He thought that she was in awe of him because he was the White Tiger. Rumours ran riot about the voyages of the White Tiger. He was a foreigner who had ingratiated himself with the Ming Emperor. He had risen from a mere seaman to an officer, up the ranks to Supreme First Admiral of the Imperial Navy. He had sworn allegiance to the Chinese Empire and denounced his Manchurian roots. His commissions took him to the far west, beyond the Indian Ocean, to a land where men's skins were as black as the earth, and riches abounded in gold and gemstones so clear and sparkling and so hard that they cut sharper than a knife. No one really believed these stories because no one had seen these lands or these riches before — except the White Tiger. And while the White Tiger explored these virgin lands, the pirates ransacked the coastal villages and waylaid unwary merchant junks.

Fong nodded, well pleased. "Of course, you accept. Now, rise. No wife of mine will be seen in such rags. I will have the men bring you new clothes and draw a bath so that you can wash off the evidence of our disagreement. Let it not be said that your husband is a cruel man. I am not, unless pushed to it by insolence. You will not suffer the taste of my whip again if you obey me. I do not wish to break you of your spirit. Only do not test me when my temper is hot."

"Fong," Li said with respect. "I agree with all you ask. I want to be your wife. I ask only two things in return: that you do not punish the pirate woman, Madam Choi. She is as a mother to me. When we marry—and I hope that the wedding will take place soon—she will be your mother-in-law."

"I will *not* have a pirate for a mother-in-law!"

"She turns to piracy only out of need. Her real value is in her knowledge of medicines. There is none other like her. One day we may need her gift of healing. She saved my life when the fox faerie poisoned me. She kept me from miscarrying when my son was still in my womb. Is that not a life worth preserving?"

Fong's eyes rotated half a turn. "Fox faerie?"

"Come come. Someone as worldly as yourself must have encountered the devilry of the fox spirits before?"

"Personally? No."

"Well, I'm sure I will have no trouble introducing you to her as I have no doubt I have not seen the last of her. She wants me dead. It seems everyone wants me dead." She clasped her hands together, bowed low. "Only you, my lord Admiral, do not wish me dead, and for that I am grateful and will serve you as a good wife should."

Fong squinted at her suspiciously. "What of the second thing? You have one other request?"

Li nodded. "You are a most powerful man, you have the respect of the Emperor himself. He will do anything you ask because you have made him famous in the world beyond. All travellers speak highly of the Ming ruler because of you. With this power, you can help me to save my son. He was abducted by the warlord Esen, who believes my son to be the tool of his death."

"How old is your son?"

"In a few days, Wu will be five years old."

Fong rolled back his head and snorted. "The great Mongol, menace of empires, is afraid of a baby? That's a laugh."

"Yes. But he means business. He will kill Wu unless I

find him."

"And you believe he has taken him to the Forbidden City, to your father? Then he is safe. The Emperor will not harm his own grandson."

"The warlord will use him to barter for lands or riches or a portion of the Empire. I don't know which. But he has hunted me down even before Wu was conceived."

Fong seemed to believe her and sent her away to bathe her wounds. He agreed to leave Madam Choi alone provided she came aboard and displayed her medicinal skill on Li. The pirates had not been quite caught off-guard, and some of their men were slain at the Navy's attack, but all hostilities ceased at Li's request. Madam Choi was escorted aboard, and the other pirates were stripped of their booty and their captives, and allowed to go free.

Madam Choi brought her medicine kit with her and soothed Li's wounds with a salve made from herbs and honey, wrapped a clean bandage over the lacerated shoulder and told her that the nick on her cheek would heal without scarring if she continued to apply the salve to it everyday for seven days. What did she care if it scarred. It would be a reminder not to get into such a scrape again. In the privacy of Fong's quarters, Li told Madam Choi what she and Zhu had learned of Esen's escape, and how Zhu suspected a plot to barter with Wu's life and the magic gemstone.

"What would you have me do?" Madam Choi asked. "I could sail north to the Yellow Sea, find a wide tributary and seek out Esen and kill him."

"No. Fong has agreed to take me to the Forbidden City himself, and present me to the Emperor — as his wife."

Madam Choi's eyes bulged wide, before shifting to the bandage on Li's injured left shoulder.

Li's eyes followed. "I did not agree to wed him out of terror. He could whip me a thousand times and I would not marry him if I didn't want to… But I want to." She held out her hand to block the pirate woman's involuntary jerk forward. "At the time, and even now, it seemed like the best and fastest way, first, to get the Imperial Navy out of your hair, and, secondly, to get to the Forbidden City and find Wu. As wife of the Emperor's Supreme First Admiral, the Emperor will hesitate to have me executed." She paused, and then added quietly. "Especially if I am carrying His Majesty's grandson… Also, and this is a slim also, I am hoping that Fong will fight to the death for me as the mother of his unborn child."

"You can fight for yourself," Madam Choi said with scorn.

Yes, she could fight for herself, but there was more at stake than just herself. "There is a time for the sabre and a time for reason."

Madam Choi smiled. "Your sojourn in the Etherworld was not wasted."

"I sincerely hope not. I still do not know what I have learned from that detour, nor do I understand what I am meant to do. I only know that this way I keep you whole, and I have safe and swift passage to Beijing."

"I can single-handedly slay this White Tiger and frighten away his followers."

"I know you can," Li said. "Now, you won't have to."

She rose to cover her bare shoulders with the clean red wedding robes that Fong had left for her, and Madam Choi ambled to her feet. "Why did you come back, Li, and allow yourself to be captured when you could have escaped with Lieutenant He Zhu and chased down your son?"

Li leaned forward and kissed Madam Choi on the cheek. "You had no idea that the White Tiger had spotted you."

She guided Madam Choi back on deck, and into a waiting serpent boat manned by three sailors to be rowed back to her junk.

Fong came to stand beside her, a look of pure puzzlement creasing his not ugly/not pretty features as he touched a fingertip to the place where the whip had seared her cheek. "It is almost healed," he said. The idea of which was preposterous. "How can that be?"

Li stroked the nearly smooth patch of healing skin. "Did I not say she worked miracles?"

Her eyes darted back to the sea and she seized Fong's military tunic by the sleeve. "Call off your man." One of the sailors sent to escort Madam Choi to her pirate junk had pulled a dagger on her. "I have no doubt that, although she is outnumbered three to one, she will kill all of your men. Do you want that?"

Fong's gaze followed hers. He grinned. "I think I want to see this magic healer of a female rogue live—for the time being." He motioned at one of his men to pass him the blowhorn. "It is done. Now come. The captain is waiting to wed us. I want you in my bed, as my wife, tonight."

%%%

She combed out her black hair until it shone like newly poured ink, let the locks fall over the shimmering red gown. It was decorated with pink gold, white jade and silver pearls along the neckline and sleeves. Her slippers were of black silk and fortunately were only slightly snug. Fong knew that her feet were not the Three Inch Golden Lotus standard of perfection, but she was taking no chances and tucked them under the long red dress that just covered her toes. Li's scorn for the degrading practice of foot binding must never surface while aboard this ship. She must walk as a noblewoman, floating and weightless like unreachable treasure, for that ideal evoked pity in men, and undying love. But for Li, deformed feet were nothing more than the crippling of a woman's will and her actions, and a lifetime of suffering and subservience. Mothers told daughters that tiny feet were the one aspect of their beauty they controlled; however, that only applied if you thought pain and suffering was beautiful.

Li was not unpleasantly surprised by the appearance of

her husband-to-be, who wore his official dress uniform, grey tunic and black satin trousers. The tunic had broad sleeves with black trim and cyan circular collar, and around his neck was black silk ribbon and at his shoulders were double-eyed peacock feathers of turquoise and black. Only officers who had performed outstanding service to the Empire were privileged to wear double-eyed peacock feathers.

The ceremony was short, and witnessed by several of the admiral's highest-ranking officers. They served a feast of fresh caught fish, dried scorpions skewered and dipped in a peppery sauce, apples from the Heavenly Mountains and preserved, salted plums. Li had not eaten this well in six years.

And then, the moment she dreaded came. In his quarters, after the celebration, she accepted his jade spear. There was no romantic foreplay, no sweet words. The man was a brute and took his pleasure like a beast. If she possessed a stone brick to do to him as she had done to Lok Yu, she would have gladly, but there was no escape from this ship, which was already heading north. Even if she summoned the Ghostfire to hide her while she stole a rowboat, at the speed the warship was sailing, the rowboat would have been left in the wake before she ever boarded it.

He rolled off her and lay silent, breathing hard. She detested the way he smelled after sex. His odour was sharp and animal-smelling mixed with something not quite as pleasant as the sea. When he left the bed, he pulled on a robe and sat opposite her in a chair, and for several minutes was quiet, before he spoke.

No moon shone tonight, but the faint gleam of stars illuminated his face in an eerie light.

"So, Lotus Lily, why did you marry me?"

"Because it was your will," she said, still lying on her back and staring at him in the dark.

"No. That is not the reason. You take a slap like a boy and a lash like a man, a strong man. Tell me the truth. Why did you marry me?"

"Because you are the White Tiger."

"Do you know why they call me the White Tiger?" he asked.

She shook her head, wondering if he could see the movement in the dark.

"They call me the White Tiger because we are long-lived in my family. Some stories say that my ancestors lived for five hundred years. Before they die, they spend their last years with their black hair striped with brilliant white. I am the last of my line.

"Where I come from, the people feared us. Even the Manchus—those savage Mongols on the fringes of Manchuria, those barbarians no better than Altan and his horde who only separate themselves from their western brethren by a corruption of our name—fled at the sight of us. We were chased into the barren lands to eke out a living in the wasted mountains, but my mother took me to the coast and found a merchant sailor willing to harbour me. You see, when I was born, my hair was all white. I was a freak and my village shunned me. Later, as I grew to boyhood, my hair turned black."

"So, I am right to honour you," Li said.

"I don't trust you, Lotus Lily."

"And should I trust *you*?" she asked. "You were ready to kill Madam Choi even when you promised me you wouldn't."

"Did I make such a promise? She is alive and free. And I hope I will not regret granting you her life."

CHAPTER NINE
Lotus Lily's Dilemma

Admiral Fong understood a mother's love for her son. His own had risked all to see him leave their land of persecution, and today, in the grey mountains of Manchuria the last of the White Tiger folk were gone. There was only him. *I will outlive you*, he had said. *But will he?* There were things he was ignorant of, things Li had not disclosed. Like the fact that her grandfather was a warlock and her mother a sorceress.

Did that mean she, too, would be long-lived? Her mother had died young. Decapitated, her remains had been burned to a crisp. Master Yun, on the other hand: How old was he? If the stories told about her grandfather were true, then he had lived before the dynasties, before the warring states of China united.

Li placed a hand on her swollen belly beneath her furs, to block the wind. Already she was five months pregnant. Rough seas had impeded their voyage to the central coast of Hwang-Hai, the beginning of the Yellow Sea. Li inhaled the briny air, her breath tinged with winter. The Imperial warship was still, except for the pounding waves that rocked it against its anchor. The admiral had gone ashore with his men to procure supplies and to enjoy a much-needed shore leave, but because of her delicate condition, he had refused to take her with him. She contemplated stealing a boat and going ashore on her own. From there, could she find a horse to carry her north? Too long, she had spent on this lug of a ship, and the gods only knew where her boy was. Fong had promised to get her to Beijing before her pregnancy showed, and now her belly protruded like a cannonball.

The time for action was past. The admiral and his men were returning. She could see them on the white-peaked sea:

four rowboats laden with supplies. She watched as they reached the warship and boarded, before Fong saw her and waved her inside. It was cold and he was right; she shouldn't risk making herself ill. It was bad enough that this unborn babe was hindering her moves.

Fong entered their quarters and tossed his furs onto the berth that they shared, and came to her where she sat preparing his tea at the table by the porthole.

"You were gone long, husband," Li said.

"How are you feeling?" he asked.

"I've felt worse. When I was carrying Wu, I was sick for six months. I suspect he disliked the diet of coarse red rice and fried rat."

He returned her smile, sat down across from her, and picked up an almond biscuit.

"You look thoughtful, husband. What's on your mind?"

He screwed up his eyes as he peered at her face; she had no idea how old he was. He could be three hundred years for all she knew, but she kept silent. Some things—most things—she knew not to ask. The only way she could tell that he was not near the end of his life was because his hair remained black.

Li poured the tea. Tiny jasmine flowers and leaves spilled into the cup, and settled at the bottom in a nest of white and yellow. A fragrant scent followed that, in Li's condition, nauseated her. Fong stared outside the porthole, and then turned back. "Something interesting happened when I went to the dockside tavern for a drink. A very beautiful woman came to our table and sat with us. She was almost as lovely as you. At first I thought she was flirting with me. She wanted to tell me my fortune."

"Oh?" Li creased her eyes in amusement. "And what wonderful future does she see for you, my lord Admiral?"

"It was not my fortune she foretold. She asked me when my child was due." Li's heart beat a little faster, and when she failed to react he said, "She read the tea leaves."

"You had tea?"

"No, *she* had tea."

Li was finding it a little difficult to breathe now. "She didn't follow you, did she?"

He stared at her, curious at her remark, while she strained to look outside. "Why are you so nervous, Lotus Lily?"

Li clasped her hands together under the table to still their shaking, swallowed, though there was nothing but dryness in her throat. "What makes you think I'm nervous?"

"Your eyes are afire. I've seen that look before. You had that look the day you learned you were carrying my child. Now tell me what you know of the Black Tortoise."

Li licked her dry lips before dragging her eyes wide to stare her husband in the face.

"You know that name," he said. "You know of the prophecy." His eyes grew hard as he acknowledged her reluctance. "Don't lie to me, Lotus Lily."

"I have heard of a prophesy concerning the coming of the Black Tortoise—that one day, The Black Warrior of the North would rise out of Manchuria and save the Middle Kingdom from its enemies."

"That warrior is my son," Fong said.

Li stared. Then she laughed. He was not amused, and her laughter died into a nervous titter. Madam Choi had marked her boy with the symbol of the Black Tortoise. The Chinese Empire was Wu's birthright, and as soon as possible, she must escape this floating prison.

%%%

The succeeding morning, Admiral Fong gave his captain orders to set sail. There was a change of plans. He was taking Li to Manchuria to give birth to his son, the future heir of the Middle Kingdom. Panic flooded Li from neck to knees. A sharp kick in her belly reminded her how soon the spawn of Lao Hu Fong would usurp the legacy of Chi Quan's boy. She ran up on deck, loosely draped in her winter furs. There was a pain in her belly that must be appeased.

"Please, Husband," she said. "I must go to the island of Si Hwang and find the herbs to strengthen your baby boy."

"What's wrong with him?" he demanded.

"When he kicks me, it is very weak."

"You have only been carrying him for five months. That seems to me normal."

"But you want a strong boy." Li smiled imploringly. "I *must* go to Si Hwang. Send a rowboat to take me."

"All right. If you need these herbs, you may get them. But I will take you myself."

"No. You mustn't waste your time. You have more important things to do. Any of your sailors can row me to the island, but they must wait while I find the herbs and brew them."

"Why can't you brew them back on board ship?"

"Because their potency will be diminished. As soon as they are cut, they must be used."

The bruised sky, ominous with cloud, promised snow or rain, and she followed her escort to the rowboat. The current was with them, and it took a mere twelve minutes for the two oarsmen to reach the island. As she climbed onto the bank, she realized she was within sight of the ship. She told Fong's men that she must go into the woods to unearth the herbs and that they must wait on the beach. Their presence—because they were male—would hinder the effect of the herbs.

"We were told to stick with you," one of them said.

"There is nowhere for me to go on an island. If you're worried that I'll try to escape, don't be. I would drown."

The man shrugged and his companion agreed. Neither wished any part of women's magic. Li thanked them when they permitted her to forage on her own, and left them by the rowboat. She hurried into the leafless forest. The herbs she needed were wilted from the cold. Fong had not questioned her even though he was well aware that winter's touch had killed most growing things. But underground, the roots she needed to kill Fong's baby thrived. It was not for nothing that she had spent all those days and nights with Madam Choi and Po, whose collective knowledge of medicinal and poisonous plants was unprecedented.

With a sharp knife, Li cut away at the woody tubers until she had three solid knots. She carried them to a glade and placed them on the ground. She drew a small iron pot from between the folds of her furs, and crouching, sparked a fire with a flint-stone amidst a clutch of leaves and twigs. She selected the juiciest of the three tubers, shaved it into fibrous curls, and dropped the shavings into the pot of boiling water. She repeated the task with the other two roots, all the while hoping that the smoke would not lure the sailors into the forest after her.

She fed the flame with dried wood and twigs until the pot foamed, and a harsh, fetid odour steamed in her face. From the smell and colour of it, the poison was ready, and she needed a moment for it to cool so that she could drink without scalding her tongue.

The brew was removed from the blaze and set on the half-frozen ground, the packed soil hissing as the iron touched the cold.

Li stirred the malodorous drink with a stick, cradled the pot to her lips and held her breath. A black shadow, amidst the flutter of wings interrupted her and she gasped, sputtering a little of the liquid from her mouth.

"Before you swallow, heed my words. I know of the prophecy that has led you to this place. But tell me: Do you really know who the Black Tortoise is?" The voice was Tao's, and he had dropped from the drab sky like a giant bat, and now hovered where she sat.

The remainder of the liquid spewed out of her mouth. She rose, clenching the pot handle in her icy hands, and placed it against her distended belly. "What does it matter?"

she asked, rubbing the side of the bowl into her furs where she could feel the baby moving. "If this one is dead, he cannot be the Black Warrior of the North."

"He is still your child, Lotus Lily. You do not know the identity of the Black Tortoise. He could be Wu, your firstborn, or he could be the son of Fong."

"But if Fong's spawn is never born, it can't be him. It could only be Chi Quan's son, Wu."

"And what if the true Black Warrior of the North resides in your belly? Who will save the Middle Kingdom from the invading hordes?" Tao smiled sadly. "What if that is not Wu's destiny? You have yet to find him. He may be even now, tainted by the barbarian Esen. We do not know which path he will choose."

Wu was little more than a baby. But he was strong-willed. He was far older in experience than he was in age. And talking to him, anyone would mistake him for an older boy in a very young body. "If he can, he will not choose to follow Esen," Li said fiercely.

Tao studied her. His only concern was that she not murder an innocent. Li squeezed her eyes shut. *Was* she a murderess? Could she take the life of the unborn simply to further her first son's destiny? Her head ached. "Please, Tao. Just take me away from here. I must find Wu. I don't really want to harm this child, but I must find Wu."

"I cannot take you anywhere. I am a hopping corpse." He raised a withered hand that looked like skin over fleshless bone. "I can fly, but I can carry no burden lest we both plunge into the sea."

Already, the iron bowl felt cold, and if she did not imbibe the deadly broth in the next few minutes, its potency would fail. The saliva rose in her mouth as she contemplated her choices, nausea filled her throat, and she could feel the baby stir. "I wish I had more courage," she said bitterly. "I wish I was more like Madam Choi. *She* would know what to do."

Something had changed in Tao's piercing gaze. His eyes were no longer black as ink, but milky. "Yes, look into my face, Lotus Lily. See what you see. I am neither alive nor dead, but my body begins to rot. Soon my hair will turn to frost to match my eyes, and my skin will gleam virescent. You are afraid of me, aren't you?"

Li felt her insides recoil, but outwardly she remained stoic.

"What makes you think you lack courage, Li? You stand here facing an undead man, and you do not run. Doesn't that take courage? Madam Choi fears nothing because she does nothing that frightens her. She has been toughened by the realities of her existence. Nothing she does is hard for her. She turned her back on her rice farming family and married a pirate. Since the death of her roguish husband, she has taken up where he left off. All that she chooses to do is what she has already done. How can she be afraid when the outcome is known to her? She has seen the worst of life and death. It is only when one is afraid that one has courage."

"I am very afraid," Li whispered, swallowing dryly. "If I don't kill the White Tiger's spawn before he is born, he may kill my dear Wu."

"Why should he do that?" Tao asked. "They will be brothers—if he is indeed a boy."

"He is a boy. A fortune-teller has confirmed it."

Li lowered her eyes to the cooling brew. "His father, Lao Hu Fong is not Chinese. He is a Manchurian under the service of the Empire." Li suddenly glanced up at him. "How did you know I was here?"

"I told you, Lotus Lily, I have been watching over you."

"Why didn't you show yourself sooner? Before this happened?" She slapped her stomach, and then regretted it as the baby kicked back.

"I cannot come and go as I please. I need nourishment. I cannot find that at sea. You were near enough to land that I could seek you this time."

"But if you were watching me, you should have been watching Wu. He was taken by Esen to the lagoon where he was conceived. You could have gone there and protected him."

"That was not my destiny." He threw a hard look at the poisonous soup that Li still clutched to her chest. "What choice do you make?"

She followed his gaze with her own, and overturned the pot, allowing the ill smelling liquid to spill onto the fire—drowning it in a seething mist.

%%%

"Things have changed, Lotus Lily," Fong said. "The welfare of my own son must take precedence. You are weak and grow paler daily. I will take no chances with my boy. If you are correct and the Mongol Esen and the fox faerie still seek your demise, I must make certain that my son is born safe. We go to Manchuria, to the foothills where the mountain folk will keep you safe. I've had news that the Empire is at risk. The Manchus threaten the northeast border, while the Mongols scratch at the west. The Emperor is up to his eyeballs in war, and has no time to deal with a fugitive princess or a new son-in-law. Especially since that son-in-law is Manchurian. I must wait to see how the tide flows. Those hateful savages have tainted the Manchurian name, and if the Manchu threat is real, His Majesty might see me as a traitor or a spy simply because we hail from the same land. I will be slandered. His right-hand man, Military Governor Zheng Min and I have never seen eye to eye."

"But you promised!" Li said, tears spiraling down her cheeks. "You promised to help me find Wu." Li bit her lip to control any further outburst. She clasped her hands together to still their trembling. The baby kicked and she wanted to kick it back. How she regretted the course of action she had so ignorantly chosen. Fong was going to hole her up in a Manchurian cave to give birth on foreign dirt like a goat—with strange Manchurian peasant women for midwives!

Why had she listened to Tao? She should have followed her heart. Her heart was with Wu, Chi Quan's son.

Fong's eyes were on her and Li was careful not to give away her thoughts. If he suspected her rancour for his child, he would imprison her until the deed was done—and his heir was born. Li gathered her composure to nod in mock compliance. "Of course. His Majesty cannot be trusted. But what makes you think your own people will harbour your pregnant wife? You say they shunned and persecuted you in your youth."

"That was three hundred years ago. All those who remember the birth of the White Tiger are dead. If the Manchu forces are a true threat and have taken the easternmost wall, then the Manchurians will welcome the sign of the White Tiger." Fong turned his hand palm-down to display the tattoo on the back of his hand. "Only a true Manchurian warrior can sire a White Tiger."

Li shut her eyes. Her husband's loyalties were dubious. If all of this were true and he could switch from one side to the other depending on who was winning, then he was no better than Jasmine.

A knock came at the cabin door.

"Enter," Fong said.

The door slowly opened and a young seaman appeared on the threshold. "I have news, Supreme Admiral," he said. "An Imperial messenger has sent word that a rebel warrior by the name of Zi Shicheng threatens to take down the Empire from within. Altan is at the Jiayuguan pass, flanking the desert sands, and the Manchus cover the east at Shanhaiguan."

"What orders?" Fong demanded.

"To quell the pirate resurgence in the south. Much needed silver is being stolen by the rogues from transport junks. Silver that is needed to pay wages and arms for the war."

"Where is the messenger?" Fong asked.

"Already gone. His Majesty needs him at home. A serpent boat took him back to his ship. But he left you this." The seaman passed him a bamboo scroll, dense with Chinese characters. The admiral skimmed the message before following him out to the deck, leaving Li pummeling the air with her fists.

Was Admiral Lao Hu Fong trustworthy? And why did she care? She owed nothing to an empire that wanted her dead.

She spooned her hands to the huge burden that weighted her belly. She might not be able to act right now, but there was nothing wrong with her ears. She had heard rumours among the officers of Fong's ship that China was degenerating into chaos. Disloyalty and incompetence were the inevitable result. She had heard of this rebel Zi Shicheng. He had started out a loyal man, but as the walled garrisons of the frontier became depleted, his troops grew weary of fighting a losing battle. Now his army marched east toward the capital, and with only one man to guard every few miles, the defense of the northeast at the critical junction of Shanhaiguan depended on one great general. That general, Li knew, was Supreme Brigade General Chi Quan.

Li had heard of Quan's latest promotion that had come through his military prowess at the frontier walls and through the abrupt departure of some of the Ming army's most senior commanders. When the Manchus began hostilities on Ming forces in the northeast, they attacked the great garrisoned loop over the north of Shenyang before moving south to exchange arrows at the Yalu River. The Manchus were picking off the remote border garrisons one by one and reclaiming what they insisted was Manchu land. Li clutched her fists in tight balls and squeezed them. There was no doubt the Manchu threat was real.

CHAPTER TEN
The Chinese Rebel

Zi Shicheng was only one of many defectors that were shrinking the Ming army in the Northeast. He had seen it with his own eyes. After years of faithful service, it seemed the Forbidden City had forgotten him and his troops. When the fort at Fushu fell, he had bolted. There was no deflecting the Manchu warriors who were superior horsemen and bowmen. No longer did the Tower for Suppressing the North, nor the Gate at Which the Border Tribes Come to Pay Homage stand. Nothing remained but broken bodies and blood, and rotting earth ramparts. He had tried seeking refuge further south.

He glared up at the night sky—a fist raised to the Pole Star—and openly denounced the Emperor. His requests had not been answered. Frozen, wet and abandoned, the morale of his troops had plummeted. The frontline of defense was manned by sentinels numbering in the thousands, but as the men wearied and died from cold, starvation, disease and battle, few came to replace them—and more defected. The fortresses dotting the Northeast stretch, west of the Yalu River were deserted. Those unfortunate enough to be stationed beyond the reach of these feeble shelters did guard duty exposed on stout towers built of solid earth.

Zi Shicheng was one of these unfortunates. This last spell of duty had him and his troops still in the frigid frontier with the weak promise of padded trousers, fur coats and boots. But had any of these items materialized? No. His men huddled in mouldy, ill-fitting clothes, their shoes worn through the soles, their hands unprotected, so that every man bemoaned the sting of frostbite. The Emperor's wall builders had not reached the Sino-Manchurian border and no refurbishment had taken place. The walls were disintegrating with each attack and suffered from the battering of wind and rain. For years, this neglected part of the Empire had been prey for the Manchus. They had systematically broken down the barrier, stripping bricks and wood for their own use. The moats were filling in with wind-blown sand. Forts were missing their gates, and it was near impossible to move on the ramparts of the wall. Those who tried often slipped and were left dangling, their feet swinging into oblivion.

"Commander," a soldier whispered, nodding past the remnants of a stone battlement. "Manchu warriors to the east."

"I know." Zi Shicheng did not dare raise the alarm with smoke signals or cannon fire. The towers were so vulnerable that cooperation was more appealing than resistance. He swung an arm to a crumbling rampart and hurled his body after it to land on the precipitous surface. He rose to his half-soled, worn-booted feet, stalwart, facing the horsemen who marched cavalierly toward the gate. Above it, legs braced apart and hands on his hips, he stood with weapons loose by his side — to show the approaching legion that he meant to barter, not fight.

"We intend to pass," the Manchu general called out. "If you do not comply, I will deploy my army to fight, and you and all of your men will die."

"If we fight," the rebel said, "some of *your* men will also die. Although you outnumber us in manpower and in armament, I think you will agree that we need lose none of our soldiers? All we ask for your free passage is a share of your food and drink, and any furs you can spare."

The general glanced at the lacerated, ragtag mess of Ming soldiers at the wall and laughed. "So be it. We feast and drink tonight."

%%%

"Majesty," Zheng Min said. "I think you will want to hear what the Mongol has to say."

"Who is this filthy barbarian and what does he want with me. All of the Middle Kingdom is in jeopardy and you bring a savage and his boy into my presence?" The Emperor twisted his head in a frantic attempt to search for his advisors. "Where is Jasmine?"

Esen glared at the military governor in annoyance. "No one has seen the lady in many—" Zheng Min stopped himself just in time. His Majesty was not himself, and had spells of forgetfulness that made him oblivious to Jasmine's long absence. But if he crossed his liege on a bad day, it could mean his head. The Emperor still had that much power. Zheng Min shunted the Mongol warlord and the boy toward the door, and whispered, "Wait in the audience hall. His Highness will see you shortly."

The boy looked strangely familiar and yet Zheng Min was sure he had never seen him before. But if what the warlord claimed was true, then that explained all. "Sire," he said, when the two had left. "You must listen to the barbarian. He may have a way for you to save face."

The Ming economy was near collapse. A Dutch blockade, a Spanish clampdown on exports of Acapulcan silver, and political turmoil in Indonesia, making the seaways treacherous had drastically reduced the flow of silver to the East. The theft of silver by pirates off the South Coast compounded the problem, and had virtually halted the export and import of goods from the Empire. "The peasants refuse to be conscripted to replace the troops decimated at the frontier," Zheng Min said. "They would rather die than fight because their crops will fail without them. And their crops *are* failing anyway, because they can't afford the taxes."

"So what do you expect me to do about it? They must be taxed. How do you think you get your mighty wage if not by taxes?"

Military Governor Zheng Min had better watch his step because if he pushed too far, he could end up with his head on the end of a pike. "The Mongol Esen has a gemstone that can see military strategies of our enemies. He claims that it is the property of your banished warlock, Master Yun." He decided to omit Esen's claim that the boy was His Majesty's grandson. If he had a grandson, he would have an heir. And the only heir that Zheng Min wished for His Highness was himself.

"Yes, I remember he used to wear such a gemstone, a ring. Where is he now? Bring him to me."

"No one knows where the old man is. Jasmine has gone to seek him."

"She has been gone long," he said, remembering now that years had passed without the fox faerie by his side. Too long, Zheng Min thought, feeling the tug of lust at his groin. "All right," His Majesty said. "Send in the Mongol. Let me see this ring."

The military governor went to the audience hall and beckoned the Mongol to wait at the door while he took the boy aside and dropped to one knee. "Do you know who I am, boy?"

The frightened child shook his head.

"Do you know who *you* are?"

"I am Wu," he said. "Son of Li."

"Li is your mother? Tell me: what else do you know about her?"

"She is a princess. My great grandfather is a warlock and my father is the famous general, Chi Quan, though I have never met him."

Zheng Min's heart raced—Quan's son? He took the boy by the chin and looked into his eyes. The steely gaze was there. The boy wasn't lying. Li was Lotus Lily? That meant she was alive and Quan was her rescuer—but how to prove it? If he could prove it, that would be the end of Quan's career. "You have never met your father?"

The boy shook his head.

"You mustn't tell His Majesty any of these things," he

warned.

"Why not? My mother is his daughter. She told me I am the Emperor's grandson."

The little fellow was smart for one so young. "You must keep it secret because he wants your mother dead. He will have your father killed if he knows of your existence. Your parents betrayed the Empire, and their punishment is death. What was your name again, boy?"

The boy's eyes grew as round as water chestnuts. "Wu, sir."

"Do you promise me, Wu? That you will keep this between us? I promise to protect you."

Wu stared at him, uncertain. That uncertainty told Zheng Min that although the boy spoke like an adult, he was only a child. Wu nodded.

"Good. Now, come with me. You must earn your keep and His Majesty's respect by keeping this secret and showing him how the Tiger's Eye works."

They passed through the twin yellow pillars and their guardians, the stone Lion Dog statues, and knelt before their sovereign. The warlord touched his forehead to the floor, then raised it and waited for permission to speak. The Emperor gave it, and the Mongol removed the ring from around his neck by unlooping the string. He kept it clasped in his hands. "First, Your Majesty, I need your word that you will pay me my ransom for this gemstone and the boy."

"Impudent savage. What do I want with your Mongol boy?" the Emperor asked.

Before he could answer, Zheng Min silenced Esen with a look. The military governor said, "The boy is of value because it is only for him that the stone speaks."

Esen's mouth dropped open; he was shot another sharp look. *Later*, Zheng Min's eyes warned. *The boy's identity is worth more to me than it could ever be to this old king.* The warlord scrunched his eyes in suspicion; the exchange between them went unnoticed—His Majesty was fixated on the Tiger's Eye.

Wu looked to Zheng Min, and he asked the warlord to give the boy the gemstone. The boy held the ring in his fist then uncurled his hand. All eyes dropped to the Tiger's Eye, but Zheng Min's own suspicious mind noticed the black marks on the small boy's palm. A tattoo? What could it mean? He wasted only a few seconds pondering it before the gemstone swirled and curdled in the boy's hand. An image surfaced from the stone. A soldier in tattered uniform with the torn armband of yellow triangle and green dragon dragged in the wind; and beside him, seated by a fire, a general of great daring, in Manchu raiment, slurped liquor from a skin bladder. They shared hot steamed buns and passed the bladder from one to the other while smoke smouldered from their fire, obscuring the face of the rebel. Laughter cackled between them. The general reached for the rebel's arm and ripped the remaining flap of armband, sending it fish-tailing into the dark. And the rebel threw back his head and roared.

%%%

A young captain stood before Quan recounting the grievances of the watchmen. He had unanswered requisitions and letters on ragged scraps of parchment; they didn't even rate the official status of bamboo scrolls. "There is no rigid timetable for border service, no set schedule upon which guardsmen can anticipate. Look here. Names. Ranks. Time served. Four months, three months, ten days, nineteen months. How can these soldiers' families survive when they don't know if or when their fathers and sons will come home? Some have been here for years. They are entitled to Leave."

Service on the frontier was torture. But it was not in his hands to change it. The Mongols were nipping at their heels. With every fort they took that the Chinese reclaimed, the Mongols succeeded to another. They were wearing down the Imperial troops, like a river eroding its banks. Brigade

General Chi Quan could not keep up with the demands of his men.

"This is war, Captain," Quan said. "We have work to do. The walls between Ganzhou and Lanzhou have been torn down to shoulder height. Our archers can only hold them back for so long. The barbarians will breach those ramparts if we don't do something fast."

The captain bowed and returned to his unit while Quan stared at the mess around him. If only Zhu were here by his side. He could use his help, his trusty sword arm, and most of all he could use the sight of the Tiger's Eye.

Where would the enemy hit next? His troops were ever shrinking as he deployed them to outposts along the border wall. What were the Mongols plotting? Divide and conquer?

Altan was a clever strategist, smarter than his brother. Esen never strategized, and merely drove his horses and bowmen headfirst to plough down his adversaries. But when hit came to crunch, Esen preferred to barter than fight. He would rather kowtow to the Emperor to receive gifts of silver and silk than clash swords for them. Altan on the other hand was taking advantage of the turmoil that was tearing the Middle Kingdom apart. Already there was talk of men deserting the outposts, trading with the barbarians for dried squirrel meat and a wolf's pelt. Quan could not be everywhere at once. Where the devil was Master Yun?

The old warlock was not here to advise him. He Zhu was not present to lend his crossbow. Quan decided that failing the help of the Tiger's Eye he would risk contacting the *yebushou*. The *yebushou* were moles. They were slippery. They worked at night. They bolstered the defensive work on the wall, making night-time sorties into enemy turf disguised as Mongols. Their job? To detect and sabotage planned raids and rebellions, even to the point of turning assassin. Unfortunately, many failed to return, content to remain on the winning side.

Quan walked several paces down the border wall to a

place that was quiet and unmanned, threw off his fur hood to reveal his red-tasseled helmet and put two fingers in his mouth to whistle. The Mongol camp was below the rise; the wind was with him, carrying the sound. He listened, then took a bone flute from his furs and piped a haunting, not quite Mongol tune.

He played for five minutes and waited. Then he blasted three short spurts.

Fifteen minutes later a sound scrabbled at his feet, and Quan dropped below the rampart to admit the mole through a tunnel built into the rock. The *yebushou* was called Ma Low. He shook off a few flakes of snow from his fur cap, and lowered it to reveal his grim face.

"What news?" Quan demanded. "Where will the Mongols hit next?"

"Datong. In eleven days time."

"We can never get to Datong in time to warn the sentry there."

The mole shrugged. "I will do what I can to detain them."

"How many ride?"

"Too many. Many thousands."

Quan swallowed. He must send His Majesty word that he needed more soldiers.

%%%

The Emperor snatched the gemstone from Wu, and the vision vanished. "Bring it back," he demanded, and shook the ring, shoved it onto his finger and commanded it to reveal its secrets. Nothing happened. He tore it off his finger and threw it at Esen. "Make it work."

"Only the boy can open its eye," the warlord said.

"Then slice the boy, finger by finger, until he makes it work."

Military Governor Zheng Min stole the boy's frightened gaze. "Best do what His Majesty desires, else you will suffer at his hand."

"I don't know how."

The Imperial yellow silk sleeves flapped at the boy. "What do you mean you don't know how? We all witnessed your sorcery!"

Zheng Min threw Wu a warning glare, and the boy's sharp eyes jerked askance for a second, before he lowered them to the marble floor without speaking.

"Show me the face of the rebel who plots the downfall of my throne!"

The gemstone in Wu's hand remained a hard yellow-brown, as inert as a frozen pond.

"The boy is frightened, Your Majesty," Zheng Min said. "He needs to rest and eat. Later, I am sure he will show you what you ask to see."

Wu was led away by a palace eunuch, and when Esen started to follow, the Emperor detained him. "You are an enemy of the Middle Kingdom. I order your removal from my court by beheading."

That got a rise from Esen who jerked up from his complacent mood. "I've brought you a gift much more valuable than the Tiger's Eye. Don't you wish to know who that boy is? I have knowledge that you have been seeking for many years, news concerning your daughter Lotus Lily—news that may change the course of this war. If the people know that you have an heir—"

"Warlord," the military governor cut in. "What gibberish do you speak? We have searched the mountain and plain for her. We all know that Lotus Lily is dead." His apprehension as he pushed his lies went undetected by His Majesty—but not by Esen.

"She is not dead," the warlord said. "Merely corrupted by pirates."

Zheng Min's brows shot up and His Majesty's mouth dropped open. "Who was her rescuer?"

The effect the news triggered bolstered the Mongol's bravado. "What guarantee do I have that you will not kill me after I give you the information you seek?"

"None. Do you think a mere barbarian can dictate to me conditions? You raise your bow to me and you are already dead." The Emperor sent his eyes to the sentries posted at various spots around the room. Fully armed, they raised crossbows, all aimed at Esen.

"Only I know how to make the boy open the eye of the gemstone," Esen said.

Was he telling the truth? Of one thing Zheng Min was certain, the barbarian had knowledge that might advance the military governor's position. The boy was also a weapon that could be used against Brigade General Chi Quan—for the time would come when Quan must be removed from the picture.

The Emperor exchanged concerned glances with Zheng Min, who bowed. "Your Majesty. You have far more important matters to attend to. I will deal with this barbarian. It is obvious that he has information that we need. I will torture him as I tortured the traitorous eunuch who defied you. I will get all of the information out of him. I promise."

"No!" Esen yelled, proving to all that he had degenerated into a coward after his long tenure away. The warlord kicked and thrashed as sentries seized him by the armpits and dragged him to the dungeons.

"Do not trouble yourself with this trifle, Majesty," Zheng Min said. "I will take care of it." He bowed, and followed the prisoner out.

The cold stone walls deflected the chill air back at him as he descended into the dark light of the dungeon. The click of heavy boots resounded on the stone floor. He ordered the guards to manacle the barbarian to the wall where he had once held Lotus Lily's tutor, Tao. The snick and clank of metal clasps ensured Esen's bondage, and he dismissed both of the guards.

Fear gleamed in the Mongol's black eyes.

Cooperate or suffer torture. It was the warlord's own choice.

"Stop your sniveling, barbarian," Zheng Min ordered. "If I didn't know you in your heyday, I would think you were a woman. Get up. Stop slumping there like an ill-hung tapestry."

His wrists were shackled, but his feet were not, and the military governor stood just beyond kicking reach. Zheng Min picked up a length of chain and rolled it noisily on a stone table, feeling its weight. Not too heavy and not too light, just the right weight to tear the flesh and beat a man blue. Not heavy enough to crack bones. One smack with this would give him the Mongol's undivided attention. Little blood would ensue, and most of the bleeding would occur under the skin. *Let's hope it doesn't come to that.*

"Now, I want the whole story," he said crisply. "Where did you find the boy? How do you know his father is Brigade General, Chi Quan?"

"Brigade General?" Esen echoed.

The chain fell with a clatter to the stone table. "That's right. You wouldn't know about his latest promotion. You've been off in the bush on a wild goose chase... And, it seems, you have found the goose." He paused for emphasis. "Tell me, where is Lotus Lily?"

"I found her among the pirates off the coast of Fukien province."

All of the Emperor's army and all of his men couldn't find the slippery princess. But this savage of the steppe had. Zheng Min masked his disgust and resentment. He made his voice flat and noncommittal. "So, the strange warrior in ancient armour was Quan, and it was he that rescued her."

Esen shrugged. "Maybe, maybe not. Of that, I can't be sure. I only know that Lotus Lily claims the boy is her son."

"And where there is a son, there is a sire. Of course, the father is Quan. The boy said so himself. Who else could it be?"

"I saw four figures with her atop First Emperor's tomb, but I was too far away to discern who they were. Only one was I certain of. And that was the warlock. I could see his grey robes billowing in the wind. I shot at him but killed another. If Quan lives, and is now Brigade General as you say, then the man I killed was not he." The warlord rubbed his grimy chin on his shoulder, as he dug into his memory. "Who else went missing that day?"

Zheng Min ravaged his own recollections of that day. Who else? He drummed his fingertips over the icy links of the chain lying on the stone table. Who else vanished without leave that day? Lieutenant He Zhu. Although the rescue was swift, the horseman who had swept Lotus Lily to safety must have been him. The rider was fast, a skilled swordsman, larger in build than most Ming soldiers, and he wore Imperial colours.

Where had He Zhu been hiding himself all these years? Traitors, he thought—all of them. He had only to prove it. But all of the Middle Kingdom was in flux. Its borders were precarious, and now the Manchus had chosen the worst possible time to attack the crumbling walls of the Northeast. The worse case scenario was that the two barbarian empires would join forces, and if they won, who would rule? This must not happen. His Majesty was weak, unable to rally the peasants to fight. They would all rather run and hide, and wait for it to be over. And then, at the end of it, suffer the domination of their conqueror.

Not acceptable.

Zheng Min turned to the barbarian. "What is a piece of the Empire worth to you, warlord? Will you join the Ming against the Manchus? Will you fight against your own brother who has usurped you in your absence?"

"The Manchus are no friends of mine," Esen said.

"And your brother? What of Altan? Are you content to go back to Mongolia, crawling on your hands and knees like a worm escaped from the crow's beak, in the hopes that your brother will take you back and allow you to be one of his lieutenants?"

Esen's face reddened with rage, and he tried to slam a fist onto his thigh, but only succeeded in wrenching his wrist in the manacle, and wincing in pain. "I serve under no one. The Mongol empire is mine!"

"No more, barbarian. Altan has the loyalty of your warriors. Has that magic gemstone not shown you the truth?"

By the slump in his cheeks and the fire in his eyes, the military governor knew the warlord was fully aware of his nonexistent status. "Altan wreaks havoc on the Northwestern frontier. He tears the walls down as quickly as we repair them. His men fall to the Ming only to rise again as if by magic. And magic, I think, is involved. Where is the lady Jasmine?" Although Zheng Min hated to admit it, even to himself, he had no doubt that the fox faerie had deserted His Majesty and taken up with Altan. "Your brother has the magic of *Huli Jing* on his side. And as far as they are concerned, you are dead."

"I am not dead!"

"Then fight with us. Even though Altan has mesmerized hundreds of thousands to his side, surely you can win back the faithful. That creature you ride—*Fenghuang*, the Chinese Phoenix—is a mount fit for an emperor. And yet, only you control her. Why is that, Esen? You have brought us many weapons, weapons of great power. But I will take them away from you if you do not comply with my design. We will find a way to use these weapons even without you. So what do you say? With your army, and the might of the Ming, we will crush the encroaching Manchus who menace the defenses around Beijing. When the capital is secure once more, the Imperial Army will help you defeat your brother and take back your horde. In addition, I promise you land in the north and luxuries beyond your most avaricious dreams."

Esen wasn't stupid and Zheng Min could see the wheels of his mind clicking over the offer. Thrusting himself forward from the dungeon's frigid walls, he asked, "And how, pray to the gods, do you intend to convince the Emperor to parcel out his land to those he insults as savages and barbarians? I've just seen how faithful his sentries are in that gaudy yellow cage he calls a throne room. He will never agree to those conditions."

"Not your problem, warlord. I will take care of it."

Esen's cold, black eyes grew as wide as those of a giant carp. His visibly dry lower lip cracked to emit a seep of blood. Thirst was almost as torturous as a beating. This man was close to breaking.

"All this talk I hear concerning a rebel insurgence," the Mongol uttered softly, eyes severely narrowing. "I believe I am witness to a plan." His voice got loud as he spat out his accusation. "The Emperor wishes to see the face of the rebel? He has only to look at his right-hand man."

"Keep your mouth shut, warlord. His Majesty will never believe you."

Zheng Min paced the floor of the dungeon, his heels echoing on the stone like metal. Using the chain on the barbarian was utterly tempting, but he refrained. "Brigade General Chi Quan is the man who stole Lotus Lily from you. His demise and a golden future for yourself are my most sincere promises. You give me your word and I'll give you mine. What do you say, warlord? I know the thirst you are feeling. Shall I send for a cup of rice wine so that we might drink on it?"

CHAPTER ELEVEN
The Pirate Truce

After everything Li had done, the Imperial warship was returning to the pirate lair in the South China Sea. Admiral Fong intended to wipe them out. So his loyalties remained with the Emperor. But what would happen if the tide of war took a drastic turn? *Does it mean that much to you for your son to be the new ruler of China?* Not going to happen, Li thought. Not if she could help it. This child, this unborn boy in her womb, the Supreme Admiral's own son, would save the pirate leader from his ruthless clutches.

Li was six months pregnant. She was useless burdened like this, and she had to rid herself of the burden without harming him. She knew just how.

Before Tao left her on that bleak and miserable island, he had taken a broken reed and soaked it in the poison she had spilled over the fire. Some of it had slopped onto the icy ground. Before the spill froze, he had sopped up some and stoppered it in the reed. Though by now the liquid was completely absorbed into the reed's fibres, it was still potent enough if she chewed on it to release its cleansing effects. It could no longer kill the fetus as the fresh brew would have, but it could induce early labour.

Tao had made her promise not to use it except under the direst of emergencies. Li could think of nothing more dire than this. At this stage of her pregnancy the mother would suffer more than the child. Her life was as much at risk as his. Did she dare?

Li dug into the toe of her shoe where she kept the slim, stoppered reed. It was the thickness of the tip of a chopstick and the length of her baby finger. Live or die. She must take the chance. Every other time she had been required to make a life and death decision, she had dived in, eyes wide open, without a thought to the consequences. Now? Now, she knew Wu's life depended on whether or not she lived. She gouged out the dead grass that plugged the two ends of the reed and shoved them into her mouth, followed by the reed itself, and chewed. A horrible, bitter taste mixed with her saliva as the fibres of grass and reed formed a coarse, unpleasant wad on her tongue. She swallowed the acrid taste, before chewing some more, until she thought her stomach might heave up its contents before the poison worked.

In a matter of minutes, she was doubled over in agony, and one tremendous contraction had her toppling to the floor. A passing sailor outside her door heard her fall and cry out. He rapped at the door while Li curled into a ball. "Madam Fong. Are you well?"

"No, Seaman, call my husband. The baby is coming."

"But you're not due—"

"The baby doesn't care about schedules. Call my husband quickly. We must find the medicine woman, Madame Choi."

The sailor muttered something about a 'pirate witchdoctor' before his footfalls pounded outside on the deck. She took advantage of the silence to spit the wad of reed fibres into her hand and discard it under the bunk. Just in time, too, because a few seconds later, Admiral Fong swung open the door with two sailors, rushed to her, and dropped to his knees. "Lotus Lily, what can we do? We have no midwives."

Now was not the time to scold him for deviating from the original plan. They would have hit the Yellow Sea and met Beijing by now had he not changed his mind to return to the south coast and attack the looting pirates.

"How far are we from land?" she asked.

"Too far. From your groans and the movement of your belly, it seems the boy is ready to greet the world."

Li swallowed a gasp as another contraction sent knives

of pain into her core. "You must seek out Madam Choi, else neither I nor your son will survive this catastrophe. The last she told me of her plans, the squads were headed to Chiang-ping."

Chiang-ping was Captain Ching's headquarters in Vietnam, and to reach it, one had to travel up the White Dragon Tail Passage, which opened from the sea. The hidden pirate's den was easy to defend because its location on the river limited the size of craft that could approach it. It was very likely Admiral Fong's warship was too large. Access to the den was difficult by land, cut off from the continent by nearly impenetrable terrain. Pirate booty was bought and sold there. That was where Captain Ching would ransom the ferryboat women, and that was where he would sell their possessions and all of the loot he had taken from the sunken *Say Leng*.

Hopefully, the pirates would still be there; otherwise where else could they search? If Fong didn't find Madam Choi soon, Li and her baby might die.

"Help me get her up onto the bed," Fong order his men. The two sailors that had accompanied him each placed a hand under her arms and shoulders, while her husband lifted her legs. They laid her flat on her back, but she immediately coiled into a ball.

"What can I do?" Fong demanded.

"Find Madam Choi," Li gasped.

Fong turned and sent his men out ahead of him. He shut the door and Li was left with her agony. A spasm shook her from heel to chest and she almost regretted her impulsive action. *I will survive this*, she told herself. *I must*. She pinched her eyes tight and inhaled. This could well become the biggest battle she had ever fought. Fong's son was determined to enter the world, but how to help him? He was positioned much too high in her abdomen. She kneaded her stomach, hoping to detect his feet at the upper end of her belly.

Another contraction squeezed the breath out of her. How much more could she take? Wu's birth had been a trifle compared to this.

She blacked out her mind and thought of nothing but empty space, focused on a bright spot behind her eyes. How soon one forgets, she chastised herself. She snapped open her eyes to stare at her swollen feet. Swollen from the pregnancy, but whole, and not in pain at all. Nothing compared to the torture of having your feet broken and bound. *Practice your form like you were sparring and spar like it was a form. You are a bird, a magnificent eagle. You can fly!*

Tears wet her eyes. She must get out of this alive—if only to unite Wu with his father.

"A ship, a ship!" she heard through the cabin walls. "Flying the red flag."

The red flag. Red Squadron. That was Madam Choi's fleet. *If only they don't come to arms, if only they recognize each other before they blow one another out of the sea.*

Li braced herself and rolled off the bunk and onto her feet, dragged herself to the porthole to stare outside. The red flag was raised, a warning to the warship to stand down or risk a broadside; and at the prow the ominous figurehead of the snake-bodied, nine yellow-headed Xiang Gong ploughed headlong toward them.

Fong ignored the warning, remained on course. Madam Choi also stayed her course. Then, without warning, she fired a round of cannon. Fong returned fire, obviously failing to recognize Madam Choi's ship. If they continued this way, one or the other of them would sink.

Li clawed her way to the door and hauled herself onto the deck. Beside the helmsman, Fong was ordering another round of cannon fire. Li shouted, "That is Madam Choi's flagship. Stop firing or you will bring death down on all of us, especially your unborn son!"

She collapsed onto the deck, writhing in agony. This boy wanted out. Fong grabbed the blowhorn and shouted,

"Lotus Lily is aboard this ship! If you want to see her alive, stop your fire!"

The cannons from the Red Flag ship ceased, and Madam Choi appeared at the rail. "Why are you here?" she demanded. "I thought you had returned to the Forbidden City."

"Lotus Lily needs your help."

Madam Choi ordered her men to stand down while she took a serpent boat to the warship. Once on board, she laid Li down on the deck and examined her. "This woman must be put to bed straight away," she said. "I must take her back to my junk where I can treat her properly and ensure the birth of your son." Before he could object, she added, "I need my medicines and the skills of my daughters. I need a birthing tub and you do not have one on your ship. If I do not take her in the next five minutes, mother and child will die."

%%%

Admiral Fong scowled at the insolent men under Madam Choi's command. These south coast pirates were the worst of the lot. Not only were they robbers but they were also defectors who worked for the deposed Tay-son family, the former rulers of Vietnam. The White Tiger had been tracking them for quite awhile, and in the years that he had worked underground he had learned the ways of the pirate traitors. Ties binding their leaders and followers were based on personal alliances; Tay-son sponsorship increased their battle skills and taught them discipline, and that was why they were so hard to eradicate. Small gangs of pirates were joined under one leader, and often these leaders would join forces with shore bandits to ransack and plunder innocent villages on the coast. But when Madam Choi revived her husband's method of organized looting, the pirates got the upper hand. They plotted in the beachside taverns, joining up with huge gangs and slipping the jaws of justice.

For many, social mobility on land was denied them. But

as pirates in an organization they could have rank, wealth and prestige. He knew even before meeting up with Madam Choi, what the Tay-son called her: Queen of the Eastern Seas. And this Captain Ching, he was better known as the King-Who-Pacifies-The-Waves. The Tay-son confirmed military rank upon these rogues and gave them incentive to rob and plunder, and although Fong knew this was a temporary survival strategy, they who began their careers as destitute fishermen and labourers, now had a way out of endless poverty.

The promises of the Tay-son were too attractive to ignore, and even in the short time that Fong had been away from the pirate waters, unstable leadership in the Vietnamese court had made smugglers of Chinese pirates. Profits were guaranteed for bringing in Chinese wealth to sustain the former royal family. And until they recouped their stolen empire, they did not care how it was done or who helped them. At each port as Fong voyaged south from the Yellow Sea, word had slipped to him of a notorious Chinese pirate who now flaunted the Vietnamese style. They called him Mo Kuan-fu — the Pirate King.

Fong looked up from his musings and beckoned to a boy who was poling a raft between the pirate junk and his warship.

"I wish to talk to you, son. I don't mean to harm you. Your mother is birthing my son. And Lotus Lily is my wife."

The boy was Po, and his expression did not change. He stared suspiciously at the admiral, then poled his raft to the side of the ship and was helped aboard via a long rope ladder. Fong studied the thin, tall lad who said, "I will not tell you anything concerning my mother's squadrons or her associates."

"Your mother and I have formed a truce until my wife and son are back on board. I mean them no harm."

"Then what do you want with me?"

"Do you intend to serve your entire life as a scourge of

the seas?"

While Po laughed, Fong remained stern. This was no laughing matter. The pirates were strong, almost invincible and they travelled in fleets. This confederation under Madam Choi had six fleets—Red, Black, White, Green, Blue and Yellow Flag fleets. Red, he knew represented her own. When Po came of age—which could be any day now—he too, would sail under one of the coloured flags.

"You are a hunted man, Po. Your mother and sisters, too, are wanted, and if you are taken by the Imperial Navy, all of you will hang, or worse. If you are judged to be a traitor like your associate the Pirate King, you will be subjected to slicing until the living blood has drained from your body. Do you know what an excruciating torture that is? You will long wish you could stab a dagger into your heart before the ordeal leaves you dead."

Fong shook his head and laughed as Po took a step backward. "That is a warning only. I asked you aboard to offer you an alternative." He paused for a moment and let his eyes sweep over the grand structure of His Majesty's finest warship. "The Emperor is in need of fine young men like yourself. You join my ranks and I will see to it that you move swiftly to a position of power. You know the sea and the water people. You would be a great asset to my crew."

Po scowled. "My loyalty is to my captain, who happens to be my mother. She is also a descendent of Shennong, which is why you won't betray her. Without her skills, your son won't survive this early birthing. Without her doctoring afterwards, he will not survive his first year."

"I'm not asking you to betray your mother. I am asking you to declare your loyalty. I know you're a pirate. But whose needs do you serve: the needs of the Middle Kingdom or the desires of greedy, wretched social castaways who will stoop to any level to feed their avarice? Are you a Tay-son stooge? Or do you plunder for your family's survival. Think carefully, son. There's a difference."

"A pirate by any name is still a pirate," Po shot back.

"Yes, but not everyone agrees to disguise themselves as Vietnamese scum—like your Captain Ching."

"How did you know about him?" Po glanced at Fong's ink black hair which had just the tiniest traces of white bands mixed among the black. His voice turned thoughtful. "I've heard stories about you since I was a little boy."

"The White Tiger eats little boys," Fong said.

Po involuntarily winced, and Fong sighed. "But alas, you are no longer a little boy. You have a choice. My purpose is merely to warn you."

"In appearance we serve where we best benefit. In our hearts, we serve for the survival our family," Po said.

"An acceptable answer," Fong replied, and released the boy to re-join the pirate junk.

CHAPTER TWELVE
The Flight of the Tiger's Eye

The suburbs of Beijing appeared on the red horizon beyond the fields and parklands. He Zhu pulled his visor low to mask his face as he approached. The road was empty, but he dodged between the farmhouses and sheds nonetheless. Ahead, the curved roofs of the Forbidden City shone golden in the late burning sun. Li's last words tumbled in his mind: *May Lei Shen protect you.*

It had taken months to return north, and the weather had turned against him with storms slowing his progress. It was as though the thunder god were blocking his return. He marched on foot now, forced to put his lame mare to rest when she stumbled over a rock and broke her ankle. It gave him no pleasure to slice his blade across her still beating throat.

How much time until nightfall? Zhu measured the angle of the light against the straight wall of the citadel. He must find Wu. And if he couldn't find Wu, then he must go to the northern frontier and sniff out Esen.

He Zhu climbed a nearby tree until he got a clear look over the wall and the maze of palace courtyards. The throne room opened to a long, lily pool-flanked ramp that led to the public square. That way was barred to him, but he could enter via Lotus Lily's chamber. Her room was attached to one of the inner courtyards; he remembered because that courtyard was next to Jasmine's. He had a brief flash of memory, and then forced the image of the fox faerie's beauty from his mind. Whatever he did, he must avoid the archway of the main palace. Sentries were posted there. He dropped out of the tree just outside the barricaded palace, and shot a nervous glance behind him.

Since his arrival in Beijing, he'd had the unearthly

feeling of being watched. Where was *Fenghuang*? Where had Esen stabled the phoenix? With its great mass, pheasant's head and peacock's tail, it would be impossible to hide. Zhu lowered his eyes from the sky to gaze at the Forbidden City as the red ball of the sun fell below the horizon, and the curved, hat-shaped roofs silhouetted against the night sky. He walked several paces back, ran full speed and jumped at the wall, then seizing the coping with his hands, hauled himself up, dropped into the public square and followed the shadows to the rear of the main structure.

Concealed by his grey mantle, he met no sentry. He blended in with the whispering sounds and the dark movements of the night, following the maze of palace courtyards until he recognized where he was. He approached the brick wall of Li's courtyard and peered over. A light drizzle wet the white flagstones; it was near bedtime and most of the palace household were preparing for sleep. Zhu eased himself over the brick impediment and crept behind the arched bridge. Below it was a lily pond, which he deftly avoided. A splash in the night would draw sentries here quicker than a horse could sneeze. Quietly, he crossed the stone patio to a cherry tree, and from there he tried to locate Li's room. If empty and unguarded, it might be a way in.

The windows were barred shut, and there were guards: two lazy shadows in the courtyard. Someone — a prisoner — was in Li's former bedchamber. He threw a pebble to the far southeast corner to draw their attention. While the first went to investigate, Zhu skittered to the wall of the building behind the second sentry and knocked him out with a hand-chop to his neck. That should lay him out for hours. Zhu positioned his back against the wall mimicking a guard. When the first returned, Zhu stuck out his foot, tripped him and laid him flat on his back. His helmet had struck stone, and Zhu checked to see that the guard was unconscious, but not dead.

He approached the windows, peeked between the bamboo bars, and heard breathing and, every now and then, a stifled sob. He risked a glance behind him, then unsheathed his sabre and pried a bamboo bar off the window. Silence ensued and he peered inside the chamber. "Wu," he whispered. "Are you there? Don't be afraid. I've come to take you to your mother."

Rapid footfalls followed as the small boy stumbled across the marble floors to the window. "Zhu!" he said. "I'm so happy to see you. Where is Ma-ma?"

"She had to warn Madam Choi of an attack by an Imperial warship. But, my boy, you are safe!" Zhu's exuberance suddenly turned serious. "Where is Esen? Has His Majesty killed him?"

Wu grabbed two bamboo bars at either end and poked his head out of the window. "I don't think so. Soldiers took me away from him. I think they brought him to the dungeons!"

"Good. Are you well? Did they treat you all right?"

"I'm fine, but His Majesty doesn't know I'm his grandson. Military Governor Zheng Min made me promise not to tell. He said the Emperor will kill my parents if he knows. And that he might kill me, too!"

That was possible, but highly unlikely. Why would Zheng Min care? "I must take you away from here until we know the mind of the Emperor. You're alive, so that's a good sign. Where is the gemstone?" Despite the dark he could see the boy's mortification. "I see you understand why you're still alive. It's because you have the Tiger's Eye."

Wu raised his flushed face, eyes round, expecting a severe rebuke. "I'm sorry, Zhu. I stole it, but I put it back. Then the warlord forced me to steal it again. He took me with it."

"It's not your fault, son. Though, in future, perhaps you will think twice before you touch another man's possessions."

Wu lowered his head in a bow of deep contrition. Then, because he was just a little boy with a boy's brief memory, the remorse switched to curiosity. "Does the gemstone show pictures for you as it does for me?" he asked.

"You saw images?"

"War and treachery."

Treachery? A big word for such a small boy. "Come, Wu. I must get you out of here before these guards awaken." Zhu pried off another two bamboo bars until the opening was big enough to reach through and hoist Wu out of the window. He pinched the Tiger's Eye between his fingers, plucked the loop off the boy's mussed hair and draped it over his own helmeted head. "I must keep this," he said. "For now."

The boy was too slow and too obvious so he must stash him somewhere until he found them a horse. A group of vegetable carts sat parked outside the stables. Zhu seized the boy's hand and dragged him to the closest one. He moved some winter melons and root vegetables out of the way, and made a small cave for Wu to hide in. "Stay quiet and still. I'll be back soon."

He Zhu buried the boy's protruding feet with more root vegetables and a giant white radish before ducking into the stables. He must take a plain horse; a gelding with no markings would serve. He sighted the perfect steed, a drab, brown animal with unremarkable features, and moved deeper into the stables to saddle it. He was cinching the last buckle, when a squeal like a pig came from outside. He ran to the stable doors and saw five sentries dragging Wu out of his hiding place, vegetables flying. The boy refused to go, and he chucked the giant white radish into the face of one of his attackers. The soldier swore, snatched Wu by the forearm, and backhanded him into the vice-grip of his comrade.

Five armed soldiers against one. I don't stand a chance. But that had never stopped He Zhu before. He fled back inside, leaped atop the gelding and kicked its flanks, whipping out his sabre. He yanked down his helmet's visor just as he shot out the door. Straw went flying. The guardsmen swung to face him. His plan was to swoop down on Wu and snatch him from his captors, but two of the sentries cut him off. He wheeled, tried again, but the soldiers' blades battered him.

The official search for Wu was on and they had opened the gates. Now that the boy was found, the guards were trying to close them to seal the rescuer in. Zhu flew through the closing gates, a second away from the horse's tail being clipped.

So close, he chastised himself. He had wasted time interrogating the boy. They had lost precious minutes. The watchmen must have revived shortly after he and Wu escaped, and raised the alarm.

But at least he had this. He fingered the gemstone with his free hand, while the other gripped the reins like his very life depended on it. The Tiger's Eye revealed what was happening at any given moment. With this he would find Wu again. Meanwhile, he must lie low, read the gemstone's visions and learn the fate of Esen.

Hair flying out wildly behind him, Zhu rode in the direction of Master Yun's temple. When he reached the frozen gardens, he alighted and led the young gelding up the path, then paused for a moment to catch his breath. The shrine with its stone fountain was empty of worshippers, all was dusty and quiet, no one had been here in many a year. Zhu tread lightly, leading the gelding inside, and tethered him to a stone inside the secret chamber behind the Jade Fountain.

When the horse was stroked down and quiet, Zhu returned to the outer temple and stared at the jade lily pads and marble fish in the fountain's basin. Water swarmed down the rock wall, filling the basin to just full, before reabsorbing into the stone. He drank deeply from the basin, then re-entered the secret chamber. Wearily removing his mantle, he crumpled cross-legged to the floor, and slid the gemstone from around his neck. At the same moment, his horse whinnied. Zhu rose to grab its bridle. "Easy there," he whispered. "What troubles you?"

A strange sound, like the batting of wings, came from outside, and he tucked the gemstone inside his mantle and listened.

"Hush, now." He calmed the agitated gelding, patting it one more time before returning to the door of the outer temple.

Pine trees curled in the cold wind, and miniature mandarin bushes perched stiffly beneath their drooping branches. On some of the bare stems, hard green buds were starting to form.

Zhu made for the giant koi pond. At this hour, no one should be about. He shivered, having left his mantle inside, and swallowed dryly. What had made the noise? He wandered to the edge of the pond, looked down. Starlight turned the water into a flickering black mirror. At first he saw nothing, then flashes of bright orange, yellow, and white—the markings of dark-speckled fish.

The batting sound again. He looked up and gasped.

On a rock overlooking the dark, half-frozen pond stood a crane, its smooth white neck shimmering like satin. Below it sat a ring of pale pebbles. In the center, the water was so black it looked like oil. Shadows moved as the trees above bent to the wind, and a mist clung strangely to the surface.

Zhu wriggled in his own skin. *Be calm*, he ordered himself, lest the vision vanish.

The mist cleared and Zhu held his breath. The crane was gone. A giant bird with the head of a golden pheasant, the body and tail of an azure peacock, and the legs of a crane stood in its place. As it batted its wings and landed in the water, Zhu's mouth formed into a silent scream. He recognized it from the artists' paintings that hung in the Emperor's palace. Shrouded by the dusky light, *Fenghuang*, the shape-shifting Chinese Phoenix, spread its long graceful wings to touch the pond's icy banks from end to end.

If Esen the Mongol could tame the beast, then the owner of the Tiger's Eye could, too. He Zhu whistled a soft cooing sound, the same kind of sound he imitated to soothe an agitated horse. The giant bird stopped swimming and floated on the shimmering surface, cocked its head and blinked at him. What language did the creature understand?

"Come," he said in the Emperor's Chinese.

Fenghuang blinked again.

Did it understand Mongol? Esen had made it obey him, and Zhu knew a few words of the barbarian's tongue. "Come to me," he commanded in stilted Mongol.

The phoenix opened its beak and shrilled.

"No, no. Come back!" Then immediately he shut his mouth, glanced quickly from side to side and saw he was still alone. The sound of batting wings lifted into the cold wind and the giant phoenix sailed into the night.

"Stupid, stupid, stupid," Zhu admonished himself, and strained his eyes toward the vanishing bird.

If only he had not been so reckless. That bird would have made a magnificent steed. He could have rescued Wu and escaped by flight, with no sentry the wiser.

He Zhu exhaled, freezing now, his battle tunic flapping in the wind. He shook his head and walked back to the Koi Temple. In his excitement at discovering *Fenghuang*, he had forgotten his purpose: Li's little boy. He must still locate Wu and plan his rescue. He returned to the secret chamber, resumed his position on the ground, and fumbled in his mantle for the Tiger's Eye.

The stone was inert, yellow-brown, on a plain gold band. He cut the thread on which the ring dangled and slipped the band onto his right index finger, and closed his eyelids. He rubbed the stone three times with his thumb, mumbling, "Where are you, Wu?" before he opened his eyes to a yellow-brown swirl that billowed into a hazy vision. The haze parted. But it was not the image he wanted to see.

A sturdy warrior lifted wolf furs from the entrance to a tent with an air of ownership. A child giggled, and on the floor of the Mongol tent, she and a beautiful, half-naked woman reclined against red silk pillows and a gold satin coverlet. The child rolled out of her mother's arms, and playfully buried herself among the bedding. The warrior watched as a golden foxling replaced the girl, and scampered out from between two pillows, flicking nine flaxen tails tipped with white.

It had taken only an instant to recognize the mother. And the Mongol warrior? Who else? He was Altan.

The image of Jasmine grew huge. Exotic kohl-lined eyes gleamed seductively. Red lips curled over a flash of white teeth. She knew he was watching her! She rose and placed her hands on her belly. *Zhu*, she mouthed, *I have a surprise for you!*

Zhu snapped shut his eyes, and then opened them to see that he had slapped his left hand over the gemstone. The vision was gone, but the memory of it remained. What was she saying? That the child was his? He jerked himself out of his stupor. Had he sired a fox faerie kit?

Then he shook his head until he could feel his brains rattle. Was the half-girl/half-fox innocent or dangerous? What did it mean? He dared not look into the gemstone again. What he really wanted to see was where they had stashed Wu. After that he needed to find Quan.

If His Majesty wanted to torture the boy for information they would have done it by now. But Zhu was certain that torture was not in Wu's future.

He was almost certain His Majesty would not have Wu killed. He wouldn't even have the warlord killed. The Emperor needed all the weapons he could muster, and Esen still controlled the mystical *Fenghuang*.

As for Wu, he was the Emperor's grandson. His Majesty would welcome a male heir. At once a message must be sent declaring Wu's royal blood. That would keep the boy safe for now.

CHAPTER THIRTEEN
The Fall of Yulin

"Stop!"

He Zhu reined his horse in, forcing it to box the air. "Are you crazy?" he shouted at the figure that had stopped him in mid gallop. "You could have been killed by my horse's hooves."

The dark shadow standing in his path lowered its arms. It moved toward Zhu's horse and raised a hand to take the bridle.

"Tao?" Zhu asked. "What are you doing here? How did you get here? I thought you couldn't leave the crypt for long. How did you make the trip from Xian if you can't tolerate daylight?"

"That is for me to know," he said. At the suspicion on Zhu's face, Tao relented. "All right—if the movements of an undead man are that important to you..." He recounted his journey, how he travelled by night on the empty dirt roads. By day he hid in caves and vacant farm buildings and sacred temples where no questions were asked. "Several times I risked blisters to my already blistered hide when I could not find shelter. But I had to warn you."

"Warn me of what? It's too late if you are referring to Esen's insidious plan to abduct Wu."

Tao shook his head. "I came to warn you about the vision in the gemstone. Do not seek Jasmine. She wants only to trap you. If you go to her she will take your soul, and bind you to her will. Do not believe her lies."

"How do I know they are lies?"

"She is Jasmine. *Huli Jing*. Her whole existence is based on lies. Listen to me Zhu, if you go to her, she will recapture your soul and possess you."

"She won't. Now, get out of my way. I must go to her

and learn the truth."

"You know the truth, Zhu. Look into your heart. Jasmine seeks only to own you."

"I am not interested in the fox faerie. There's another I wish to meet."

Tao moved another step closer until the gelding's head rested on his shoulder, and as he stroked its mane, miraculously the fitful animal calmed. "You are lonely, Zhu. You have always been lonely. That is why the fox faerie was able to impose her will on you. You don't remember, but it's true. For a while your friendship with Chi Quan soured. Neither of you knew whether you could trust the other. But Master Yun enslaved her and released you, and now she is free and wants you back. And you have no friends to counsel you because you are an outcast for choosing justice over complicity."

"Yes, and look at where it's gotten me. I am useless here. I must go and learn whether I am a father. If I have spawned evil, then I must destroy it. As for Wu, he is safe, I've made sure of it."

"Fool," Tao chastised. "Your nephew will be killed."

"Killed? No. The Emperor would not—" Zhu bit off his own words. The significance of Tao's rebuke opened his eyes like a siphoning cloud.

"Yes, my boy. You have a nephew. A family."

"What are you talking about? And why am I wasting time talking to a dead man? Get out of my way I say!" Zhu dug in his heels and his horse whinnied, pummeled the night with its feet, almost punching Tao in the head, but still it stayed rooted on the spot.

"It senses my will and knows you mean to send it into danger. Listen to me, Zhu. I ask only that you hear me out, then do what you will."

There was no way he was getting out of here unless the hopping corpse released his horse. Zhu flapped the reins in frustration but the horse only brayed like a donkey. He relaxed his grip on its flanks, letting the muscles of his thighs slacken. "All right then. You win. Speak."

"Don't you want to know who this family is?"

"I have no family," Zhu said. "I was raised by monks — or so they say. I have no memory of my early years. My earliest recollections are at the palace where Master Yun trained me to be a warrior. I have no mother and no father. I am an orphan. I have always been alone. Until Chi Quan befriended me when we were boys." He snorted in impatience. "But what has this got to do with anything? I have a quest to complete."

"And yet, you are torn."

"I am not torn. I have made my decision. I must seek Jasmine. Wu will be safe." Zhu's eyes suddenly widened until they hurt. "Wu *really* is my nephew? But how?"

"He is. And now that you know, you must stay and save him from the evil that awaits him in the Forbidden City."

"Wu is safe. Just now I sent a message by way of a respected merchant I encountered as I left the city gates. I paid him well with silver. He'll deliver the news to His Majesty in person."

"That messenger was waylaid. Murdered by Zheng Min. He doesn't want the Emperor to know that Wu is his grandson. He has designs on the throne himself."

"How do you know this unless you are party to the plot? You've been watching me. You're a spy!"

"Ah Zhu," Tao said. "Forever suspicious; forever impulsive. For once in your life, go with your heart. Listen to what it tells you is true." Zhu caught the gleam of white as Tao's eyes rolled in exasperation. "Fine. You think I'm a spy? Good. Because I am. I've been hiding in the dungeons of the palace. And yes, I have been watching. I have been watching you ever since you arrived in Beijing, and I have been watching His Majesty's men. They are fools, most of them. For now the dungeons are empty. They never lock the doors there because no one who enters ever leaves. The white bones of the dead are testimony to that."

"*You* left," Zhu said, his voice acerbic. "When Zheng Min tortured you to get the truth of Lotus Lily's whereabouts, you escaped."

"They thought I was dead."

"And so, now you are. But that was not the question I wished answered." He Zhu sucked in a long breath. "How is Wu my nephew? And please don't tell me that I am His Majesty's long lost son, else I shall laugh—or spit—in your face."

The mockery fell short on the hopping corpse, and though the stars shed small light on his features, humiliation stained his face. For a long moment he was silent, and when he finally spoke, his voice cracked. There was scorn and recrimination, but also regret. "Ling She, the former empress, had a dalliance with a man other than her husband. This happened three years before Lotus Lily was born. So do not worry. The Emperor is not your father. Back then His Highness still led his armies against the northern invaders himself. He was gone a long time. Even when he was home, he sorely neglected her, preferring his concubines to his wife. The Empress was lonely and took another to her bed. You were the result of that union."

"Then why does no one know of this?"

"Someone does."

"Yes, well, obviously, that someone is you," Zhu said caustically. "Who else of the palace's eunuchs and women knew about me?"

"A concubine. She played midwife. Her name was Dahlia, but she disappeared shortly after your birth. I think, perhaps, the Empress paid her off to disappear and speak nothing of it. You have to understand, Zhu, if the Emperor knew of you, Ling She would have been executed."

"But she could have pretended that I was the Emperor's son!"

Tao's face grew hard, and even in the night blackness, Zhu sensed the eunuch's disapproval. "Is that how you would have liked it to be?"

No. But the knowledge of an heir would have stabilized the Empire. In all honesty, it would have saved Ling She from the horrible death that had claimed her anyway when she failed to produce a male heir.

"Your mother was a proud and courageous woman — a true empress. She refused to lie to her husband. She just didn't tell him the truth. And he never asked. Many young boys were brought to the palace household to be raised as warriors." Tao flicked a hand dismissively. "You were simply one of them."

%%%

Peng was a perfect child and like all fox faeries, she was growing fast. She knew better than to turn into a nine-tailed fox kit during Altan's strategic meetings. She slept soundly now on her bed of Chinese silk coverlets and pillows, while one of Altan's officers waved a stick over a parchment map of the garrisoned walls northwest of Beijing; they were due to take Xuanfu and Datong.

Altan paced the floor. Jasmine watched him and his generals from the corner of the tent where they had fashioned the nursery. His spies had returned from their sortie into the enemy camps. "It's simple," one of his generals was translating, "the signal towers have codes for communicating numbers in an enemy approach: one fire and one cannon salvo for up to a hundred raiders, and two of each for five hundred to one thousand. Three for up to ten thousand. And five for well over ten thousand."

"We can make them think we are less," Altan said.

The general agreed and pointed to the map of the tower placements. Some were twice the height of the wall, others nine meters high, and others half that high. There were two main types of towers: solid platforms for watching and fighting, and hollow towers where beacons were lit and supplies stored, and where some of the men slept.

"We hit the platform towers," Altan said. "They offer no shelter. Soldiers can only reach safety by heaving themselves up the walls on ropes, and in that position we can pick them off as easily as nesting ducks. We trick them into thinking there are only a few hundred of us, but we hit them with thousands." He bent to roll up the map. "Put this somewhere safe. It will come in useful."

His warriors were dismissed, and Altan stood staring at Peng who still slept soundly. Jasmine lifted the murmuring girl in her arms and rocked her, whispering, "Your daddy is coming, little one."

%%%

The birth of baby Lao was excruciating, and if it wasn't for Madam Choi's expertise and knowledge of medicinal herbs Li would have died. A week had passed since the ordeal and Fong was aboard his warship, celebrating the birth of a son with His Majesty's finest rice wine.

Baby Lao was swaddled in bamboo cloth diapers. He was nearly three months premature and weak. Li had nursed him through the first precarious week of his life and now she plotted her escape. Too much time had passed. Was Wu still alive?

She was in Madam Choi's cabin minding the sleeping infant when the door behind her opened quietly and shut. Li turned.

"I hope, after all I have done to save the life of your number two son, you are not still plotting to end his life." When Li's only response to her adopted mother's comment was to cup a hand to her mouth, the pirate chief accused her. "Your labour was induced. The only way I know to induce sudden labour is the use of a certain hardy winter tuber."

"I could not wait another three months," Li cried. "And Fong refused to take me north. He got orders from the Emperor to squash the pirate resurgence. He meant to hunt you down and all of your people!"

"We could have taken him." Madam Choi shook her head. "You risked a lot by making the choice you made. I see that spending so much time with Po has taught you a great deal. I was unaware of your interest in the teachings of Shennong. It is dangerous knowledge if used wrongly."

"I know. But I do not regret the action I took. The boy's alive. And I am free of this burden." Li patted her flaccid stomach. "As soon as possible, I must flee."

"And what of the boy? He will die without your milk. He is weak, Li. I can feed him a serum to strengthen him, but I cannot give him the protection your milk will provide."

"I was raised on soy and ewe's milk. It did me no harm."

"We have no sheep and no soybeans. Not even a goat or a hog. The Imperial Navy watches us like vultures."

"The only way we can continue this truce is to use Fong's son as a weapon," Li argued. "The admiral will not harm you or the others as long as Lao's life depends on you."

Madam Choi crossed her arms over her chest. "I will not use a babe as a shield."

"His intention was to round up your squadron leaders and send them to the capital for execution. What then would become of your children?" Li implored.

"There are not enough Imperial sailors to round up anyone."

"Backup is coming. He doesn't work alone. And the White Tiger, if you haven't heard the legend, never fails."

Madam Choi's chin jutted out as rigid as the hands on her hips. "Our weapons are no match for the Imperial Navy's, but we still outnumber them."

The boy started to cry, and Li went to his bed. The first week after the birth, she had done very little except nurse. She had been too weak and hadn't even looked at the boy very carefully. She studied him now, noted the patch of black hair on his head and the features so like his father's but softened by infancy. At least he had not been born with white hair. That would have been a disaster.

The baby formed his mouth into a circle and wailed while tears wet his pink flesh. Did he need changing? Li hoisted him from the bedding and laid him on the hard plank floor to check his diaper. Madam Choi followed her and as Li removed the wet cloth, the pirate woman grabbed her hand. "Let me do that. You're still tired from the birthing. Go and rest."

Li tried to lift the baby's leg, and Madam Choi drew her away, but not before Li glimpsed the black birthmark shaped like a tortoise on Lao's left thigh.

%%%

"Work quickly, boys." Brigade General Chi Quan's voice boomed over the scraping and clanking of moving stone and fired clay bricks. "Datong is counting on us."

He Zhu waited behind the second wall at Yulin, senses alert. His horse shuffled, and he urged it into silence. The wall builders were working on the frontline of defense, and as quickly as the Ming could raise the fortifications, the Mongols toppled them. Sometimes the barbarians stormed the barricades, ramming the walls apart with poles, before racing away. Other times they stayed to exchange blows with His Majesty's keenest archers.

The garrison was bustling with temporary kilns and mule-drawn carts, toting bricks and stone to mend Altan's latest assault. And although He Zhu longed to fight side by side with them, he felt his quest too critical to postpone. Which pass of the great wall should he try to breach? Not this one. Yulin was overrun with soldiers and workers. Discretion was crucial, but so was a brief meeting with Quan. The brigade general should know that his son was a prisoner of the Forbidden City.

Unfortunately, conversing with Quan was too risky. He steepled his hands in reverence to the south wall; then paying a silent farewell to his countrymen, left the bustle of the wall builders and dipped his horse south before turning west. His best hope was to follow a southwestern trajectory and find a spot where the wall was weak.

He galloped over the open plain, spurring his horse into the night and then the day, and then into another night and another day. To the south he caught glimpses of passing farms where the plight of the peasants put his heart to shame. Though spring was only a moon's cycle away, the land was raw and ravished and pitifully brown. Taxed to despair, come warmer weather, many farmers would not have the seed to rekindle their lands. The wall wound like a serpent, slithering from east to west, and from its westernmost extreme among the desert flats of Jiayuguan, to its eastern endpoint where it tumbled into the coastline of the Yellow Sea, every fort, rampart, crenellation and plaque in the Ming wall told of the greatness of the land over which it guarded.

He Zhu's heart swelled with pride to know that he had helped to build and protect this supreme emblem of China. He had journeyed to both ends and remembered the awe the end passes had inspired, and even though fortifications extended beyond Shanhaiguan and Jiayuguan, dwindling out into the Red Desert and winding toward the Manchurian stronghold in the northeast, the two sites were the official end passes of the border wall. Both were elaborate fort complexes with gates, towers, government offices and temples.

Most of his time had been spent at Shanhaiguan, and he had supervised the building of the main fortress, ordering the stacking of the grey-brown bricks into grim, windowless, dungeon-like walls, topped with deep, carved eaves, which overlooked the coast and the northern range. It was nothing like the western stronghold that he now glimpsed. The triple towers of Jiayuguan with their carved eaves, set within a crenellated square of walls rose over the western sands like a monument to the gods, a contrast to the black and yellow patchwork of farms he had recently crossed to reach this pass.

The outpost of Jiayuguan was still two hours ride away. Zhu reined in his horse and slowed to a trot. He came to a halt and waited. No sentries moved on the wall as he approached and dismounted. He led the gelding to a scrawny shrub, which afforded only minute camouflage, and tethered it. At first the wall gave the appearance of an impenetrable barrier, but this section was noticeably lower because no one had come to make repairs.

Where was Altan's camp? During the last raid, the Mongols were not too far from Red Salt Lake at the edge of the Ordos sands. After that bitter defeat, they had fled west to the flanks of the Gobi desert. Hopefully, they were there now.

His head popped over the edge of the wall and he hung there by his hands to get a lay of the land. The plains were laid waste here, blending into yellow-grey sand, and the wind bit harsh and cold. His mantle flapped behind him and his fingers burned with the strain of suspending his body from the wall. He blinked, snapped the sand from his eyelids and squinted. The sun created a glare on the desert and the wind dried the moisture from his eyes, rendering him as good as blind.

But something moved on the horizon. A black flood of motion, as though a hundred thousand horsemen billowed dust. Zhu gasped, touched his parched tongue to his cracked lips. A mirage? No. He could almost feel the vibration of riders, and when he dropped to the ground to pin his ear to the earth, the thunder of hooves was unmistakable. Which way would they turn when they hit the wall? Which garrison did they intend to attack?

Guyuan and Ningxia were protected by double and triple walls. If they headed for Datong, it was still a ten-day ride — even if they went without food or sleep. They must be heading for the garrison in between. Their target? Yulin, where the wall builders were making repairs. They would assault an already weakened fort, rest after they had reaped their spoils, and move on to the next manned garrison. They intended an ambush. No one would expect a raid at the same location so soon. He must return and warn Quan.

%%%

The pirates must make a living and Admiral Fong's Imperial Navy must be satisfied. How to do this? Li's baby was safe now that she intended to stay among the pirates, and nurse him herself. Lao was growing stronger daily, but Li had put Fong off by insisting the boy was still frail, and that had kept the truce between Madam Choi's pirates and Fong. But she had no control over Mo Kuan-fu — the former Captain Ching. He was gathering fleets around him, and would soon outdo Madam Choi and usurp her. Most of the pirate squads were defecting to the Pirate King, who promised them freedom and great riches. All Madam Choi had given them was a truce with the Imperial Navy and now the pirates were itching to loot.

Li was still feigning weakness, insisting that she needed Madam Choi's ministrations, and Fong was sceptical at first, but when he saw that her cheeks were ripening like apples, he decided it was not such a bad thing. One more week, he insisted, and she and his baby son must return to the Imperial warship. In one week, Li had to have a plan in place to keep the White Tiger and the Pirate King from coming to blows.

%%%

"Supreme Commander," the general called out as Altan sent a boy to water his horse. "Do you want to see the maps?"

Altan dismissed the general with a flourish. He had no more use for maps. Everything he needed to know was up here. He tapped his right temple. The Ming were coming down whether they liked it or not.

He knew where all the walls lay and the purpose of

their varying constructions. The height of walls was determined by the nature of the landscape. Walls were higher on open ground and lower on mountains where natural ridges provided a defensive advantage, requiring the walls to be no steeper than a few feet. In every type of wall construction—high, low, fortressed or unfortressed—the ground was evened out by layers of stone and brick. The floor along the tops of these walls was paved to allow horses to gallop along their length, and bricks formed crenellated battlements on top of the entire structure to provide a lookout for guards and patrolmen.

Interspersed along the wall, raised platforms, towers and forts comprised part of a tactical defense network used for observation, communication, fighting and shelter. The number and frequency of sentries on these posts depended on the security risks associated with the surrounding terrain. In some spots, towers were only thirty or fifty paces apart. Beacon stations were obvious and in sight of one another. Alarms were set off by smoke during the day, fire at night and cannon. Altan had successfully interfered with the beacon system by wiping out some of the towers, and he had yet to see it at play. But if it worked, it could set off a warning from the eastern stretches of the wall to its westernmost extreme.

Altan awaited the return of his moles to report on the codes that would tell him what these smoke and fire signals meant. He already had some inside information on the signal towers, but once he had fully cracked the Ming code, he would have the upper hand. He would shatter the Middle Kingdom. They could run, but they could not hide.

The golden fox galloped up to him and rubbed her head against his knees. He smiled. "No time for this my black-eyed vixen. What news have you brought me from Chi Quan's camp?"

Immediately, Jasmine transformed to her human form. "I have some information concerning the signal codes: one fire lit, all is calm; two fires lit, possible danger. Three fires lit, sightings of battle. We can use this knowledge to our advantage." She smiled, and looked up from watching the Mongol camp on the low plain just beyond the walls of the garrison on the north side, below a shallow ridge too distant for the Chinese watchmen to detect.

%%%

"Who goes there?" a soldier shouted from a watchtower.

He Zhu clamped his visor over his face to mask his identity, flashed the Imperial armband of yellow triangle and green dragon, the red tassel on his helmet spinning as he whipped his head to seek Chi Quan. "Where is the brigade general? I must speak to him. A hundred thousand barbarians are behind me!"

The soldier swung himself down from the tower by a rope landing at Zhu's horse's feet. "How soon?"

"Last I looked, they were a days ride behind." He Zhu dropped from the gelding and led it into the garrison. The soldier followed shouting at him to stop, but was ignored. "Quan!" Zhu shouted when he sighted the brigade general who was dispatching orders for wall repairs to his captains. "No time for restoration. The Mongols are coming. Light the beacons. We need more men!"

Quan stared at the travel-worn soldier who refused to raise his visor to show respect for his superiors. The sentry that had followed him seized his arms while another made to grab his helmet. Quan stayed his hand. "Let him be. He brings us warning of an attack. Do as he says. Light the beacons."

Quan seized Zhu by the arm and thumped him on the shoulder in a display of unbridled pleasure, stared at him exuberantly, a smile creeping over his features. "You are well, old friend?"

"As well as these times will permit." Zhu returned the sentiment, though little could be detected from under his helmet.

An unmistakable sigh escaped Quan's lips, and he led his former lieutenant into the fortress. "We don't wish to be disturbed." He threw the order over his shoulder at the soldier and added, "Anyone disturbing us will be severely punished."

Beneath his visor, Zhu grinned. Quan had never tortured a man for disobedience and he certainly wasn't about to do so now.

Zhu threw off his helmet after they entered the fortress. It was good to get the hot metal off his head and let his scalp breathe.

"The gods, Zhu," Quan exclaimed. "I never thought to see you so soon."

"I can't stay long. I have a grave mission to complete. But I saw the armies of Altan headed your way and I had to warn you. Get your men armed. How many soldiers do you have?"

"Not enough I'm afraid. There's talk of anarchy in the kingdom. I fear the signals will not be answered."

"Never mind. Fight with what you've got."

Quan clapped a hand on Zhu's shoulder. "You must stay and help. I need your sword arm and your bowmanship."

"Lei Shen knows I'd stay and fight if I could, but the fox faerie is up to mischief again and I must stop her. Only I can."

"No, Zhu, you mustn't. She will enslave you."

"Not this time. Forgive me, Quan. But if I don't face her now, the gods know what she'll do."

Quan went silent, his arm returning to his side as he nodded. "Yes, I understand. I know that what you do, you do with a pure heart. I won't stop you. Do what you must, but first tell me: have you seen Li? It's been so long since I last saw her and my heart longs to go to her, but duty keeps me at this infernal wall. Tell me she is well and still loves me."

"She is strong and courageous. You'll not recognize her when you see her again. She wields a sabre like a seasoned warrior, and kicks like an ox. You will be proud."

"Did she ask about me?"

"Much has happened since you left her in the care of the water people. Her life absorbs her." Zhu's eyes brightened. "But I must tell you this. You have a fine son."

Quan's eyes lit up even brighter than Zhu's. "A boy?"

"Didn't I just say so? And he's here, Quan. In the north, at the Forbidden City."

"With Li?"

"No. Li remains with the water people." Zhu told him of their last encounter on the beach where Esen had escaped with Wu, how they had disappeared on *Fenghuang* and reappeared at His Majesty's court. "She was compelled to return to warn Madam Choi of an impending attack by the Imperial Navy and sent me after the Mongol and his captive."

"You say his name is Wu?" That was Quan's father's name. "And His Majesty accepts him as his grandson?"

"I'm sure he will," Zhu said. "You must return to the palace to make sure he does."

Quan's face darkened and his voice grew brittle. "You just left him without knowing?"

"I had no choice, Quan. I am a hunted man for saving Lotus Lily from the executioner's blade. And now the fox faerie threatens all with this new weapon of hers."

"Forgive me, Zhu. You have done more for mine than I deserve. Won't you tell me what this weapon is that you speak of? Maybe I can help."

"No. You're needed here. And you must go to your son. I'll chance it alone." Zhu yanked his helmet over his head. "Farewell, good friend. Dream of a day when the red wheel of the sun once again floods the countryside and the barbarians are trapped in their barren lands. That day, Li will leave the Waterworld and return to where she belongs. A new emperor will be crowned and perhaps a wedding? On that day, I hope to call you brother-in-law!"

Zhu flung his mantle behind him as he turned to leave the brigade general. As he exited the garrison on horseback, he tossed a fleeting look at the fort entrance — and caught a look of sheer bewilderment on Quan's face.

%%%

Altan's armies were too numerous for the Emperor's beleaguered troops to fight. The brigade general deployed soldiers to Datong and raised the alarm. He sent five hundred men and when it looked like they could hold Yulin no longer, he gave the order to flee.

The warlord was already one step abreast of him. Altan employed the same strategy as Quan and sent half his men to the unwary garrison, while the other half stayed to fight. Datong was protected within a circle of walls, and Altan would still have to breach Shanxi before he could reach it. He must not be allowed to take it — after Datong, there was only the bureaucratic border town of Xuanfu and the poorly guarded Juyong pass before the path was clear to Beijing.

CHAPTER FOURTEEN
Datong Under Siege

"How many fires?" Altan demanded.

"One fire and one cannon salvo," the mole responded.

"Good, that means they think there are less than five hundred of us. That will make the Chinese cocky. We stay hidden and wait for the next signal. How many soldiers do they have in the garrison?"

"A few thousand at most."

Altan nodded in satisfaction, and the mole left on horseback to return to his hiding spot, which was a tumble of large rocks and discarded clay bricks overgrown with dead vegetation and a spindly mulberry tree. His location was just below the wall on the north side in a section that had no guard. Altan and his fifty thousand men were well out of view of the Ming watchtowers. He had sent a small band to camp a few miles north of the wall, but the bulk of his army was seven miles behind, awaiting the conquering heroes who had remained to seize Yulin. When these troops arrived they would storm Datong.

He could already hear the thunder of horses as the victors pounded toward his camp. Had they captured the notorious brigade general of whom he had heard so much? He would have enjoyed staying behind to finish the job himself, and meet this man of glorious story and deed, but his first priority was the demise of Datong.

As the white crescent of the moon rose with the descent of the red sun, Altan's troops reunited, and in one grand army marched to the arid plains outside the garrison. They approached by night, silencing their horses from a gallop to a canter, and then to a slow trot. From here, they were still distant enough to avoid raising the alarms. They had yet to meet up with the small band Altan had sent on ahead. He signaled his men to a halt, and his generals motioned the order down the lines of mounted, armed warriors. He raised his eyes to the black ridge winding along the distant horizon like a desert snake.

The Ming expected a raid of less than five hundred. Their signal fires were lit, a single beacon at intermittent towers, winking in the dark like yellow stars from east to west. Then a second fire lit up at each tower: a warning of possible danger. The alert was still low. They had no idea that one hundred thousand horsemen awaited. Altan directed his generals to make camp. He dared no fires for fear of the watchtowers. He ordered a cold supper of dried squirrel meat and raw winter tubers, and hunkered down on the dusty ground to scratch out a plan.

In every border district most towers were built of solid earth, and each hung a rope ladder down one side, which made access easy for the sentries. Altan's plan was to catch the sentries off-guard so that they couldn't climb the towers in time to light the signal fires.

%%%

Brigade General Chi Quan swung into the Datong garrison by way of the Shanxi pass and into the circle of walls from the south. The barbarians had not followed. Or at least showed no sign of pursuing a southern route. He alighted from his horse and handed the reins to a soldier, before meeting with the officers in charge to warn them of the impending raid.

"It's been six days since we received your previous warning, Brigade General," a young officer said. "No sign of the Mongols yet. Not here. Quingshuiying warned of a sighting of a small band passing, but they have not attacked. We've set sentries all along the walls and doubled the watches. If they're out there, they're keeping low."

That explained why the signal had been changed from red alert to amber, but Zhu had said that he had spotted a tide of a hundred thousand. Had he been mistaken? Even those that had attacked Yulin didn't number in the tens of thousands. What was Altan's scheme? Where was he? Had Quan left Yulin too soon by trusting the word of an incumbent monk? He Zhu had not contributed to military strategy in several years, had not fought as a warrior or seen the havoc Altan's barbarians had wreaked upon the Emperor's lands. Zhu had traded in his crossbow for a monk's gemstone; so as far as warfare was concerned, he was rusty.

"Don't relax your vigilance yet," Quan ordered. "The walls are strong, but they are not impenetrable."

Quan turned to enter the fortress where the officers' quarters were stationed, but before doing so, he looked to the silhouette of the Dragon Wall. He had fought the battles of the Emperor for almost his entire adult life, had conceived of the wall in the first place, and had wrestled with His Majesty's advisors on the building and linking of the individual ramparts. Was it a mistake to have taken the project so far? The Tower for Receiving Distant Nations was now dilapidated, and to the passing Mongols was no more than a symbol of Chinese decadence and arrogance. Had he been arrogant in thinking he could keep out invading foreigners this way? The military had been a shambles and it had seemed their only hope.

Now he questioned his own judgment and the years he had put into building this costly barricade. Calls for repair came so frequently that the wall never functioned effectively as a single unit along its entirety, and he had given up restoring the eastern ramparts north of Shanhaiguan. Now the sentries there were deserting. The Manchus were gearing up for an attack no less brutal than what Altan's barbarians had inflicted. Quan could not be everywhere at once, and no one was taking charge in the east. What the devil was Zheng Min doing? Why wasn't he answering Zi Shicheng's calls for help? He had heard nothing from the commander in many months.

The cost was huge. The stretch of wall in the east cost 65,000 ounces of silver, plus a further 25,000 to strengthen weak spots. Fortifications to the west cost 3.3 million ounces of silver over the past six years—well over the government's annual revenue. It was no wonder the late grand secretary, Ju Jong, had discouraged the wall building. Perhaps he was right.

Inside the fortress Quan consulted with his commanders. Men were deployed to reconnoiter the bordering plain. Nothing amiss was noted and the scouts returned. Beyond the narrow crenels of the fortress, it was quiet. "Stay on your guard," Quan ordered. "Take turns sleeping."

He himself had no intention of sleeping. Something did not seem right. He slumped his head against the back of his chair, intending only to rest his eyes a moment before ensuring his orders were obeyed. But that moment of repose cost him. He fell asleep.

Shortly after midnight, Quan woke up to the snorts of Mongol horses. He raced outside to raise the alarm, whipped about to seek his highest officers when a battle cry rang out. "Seize your bows, man your blades, we've been ambushed. The Mongols are here!"

"What happened?" he demanded of one of his captains.

The commander's face flushed with mortification as he glanced beyond, and Quan turned to face three streams of smoke pouring from the towers. While the guards snoozed like contented hogs—even though he had explicitly ordered them not to sleep at the same time—a band of Mongols had drilled holes in the brickwork with daggers and lit torches with which they'd fanned smoke through the perforated walls to asphyxiate the slumbering guards.

Quan grabbed a hanging rope and swung himself up to the platform where he could see the damage for himself. Hordes of Mongols were climbing the ropes to the towers and in the distance a black cloud, huge against the starry sky, flooded like a river overflowing its banks. A hundred thousand horsemen. Zhu was right.

"Light the beacons! Five fires. Five cannon salvos! Look alive, men. We're under siege!"

The twang of bows whined as thousands of arrows slung into their enemies' midst. It was as Quan had feared: after that first alert he had sent from Yulin, Beijing had failed to respond, and by the time he reached here, except for the five hundred he had sent himself, there were no more soldiers present than there had been before his arrival. He would have to go to the Forbidden City. The Military Governor was ignoring his messengers. If Zheng Ming would not act to save the Emperor's walls, then Quan must go to His Majesty himself.

Quan saddled his horse and ordered his men to stay their positions, to hold the garrison at all costs until he reached the capital. He would ride all night if he had to. If His Majesty wished to save his throne, he must rally his people, and send every peasant and farmer, labourer and merchant, fisherman and civil servant to fight at the wall. His lungs burned as he galloped into Xuanfu and hauled his horse to a stop. Sentries normally guarded the bureaucratic border town. Why were there none? He dropped from his mount and crept quietly up to the gates. He left his horse outside, tethered to a stout, standing stone. Where was everyone? This was the last outpost before the Juyong pass and the road to the Forbidden City.

A foul coppery smell assailed his senses as his foot hit something soft. A corpse. The copper smell was the stench of blood, and the only reason the settlement was spared a host of gorging crows was because of the dark. On the ground were signs of a raid: bodies of Ming sentinels and government officials—and Mongol arrows. Altan had split his army into three: left one to take Yulin, a second to besiege Datong and sent the third to attack Xuanfu. This last was the least of the threats. Xuanfu was little more than a village filled with bureaucrats. The Mongols had hit from the north side of the walls when Quan and all of his generals had expected a southern sequence of attacks. Yulin, Datong, and *then* Xuanfu. The barriers were positioned to protect each outpost if one was taken, but the warlord was too smart or Quan had tried to be too clever. Altan was not Esen. Esen would have gone for a southern approach while his baby brother followed the rule that the simplest strategy, even if it was the more difficult to succeed, was the best. He had stayed on the north side of the wall even though he had infiltrated the two most critical garrisons protecting the western approach to the capital—because he knew that was the last thing the Ming military expected him to do. Quan had been outfoxed. Fool, he cursed himself, but there was no point. He couldn't change what already was.

And now this. He stepped over the dead bodies and sought the governor's house. It was a smallish home, but in a small town where folk lived in tiny one-room dwellings, it was a fine and grand palace. Quan knocked on the door. He peered into a dark window and saw a white face duck out of sight. "Who's there?" a voice whispered.

"I am Brigade General Chi Quan. Where is your master?"

"Fled to the capital," the voice said. A young man in plain clothes crawled out of the shadows and peered out, then beckoned him inside.

The trembling servant bowed, recognizing a superior. "The master evacuated his family when the Mongols attacked. They got out, but they didn't have a horse for me, so I stayed. I've been hiding here for days."

The servant was barely visible because of the darkness in the house, but Quan dared not light a lantern. "Tell me quickly. What happened?"

"We weren't alerted to the raid. We saw no warning fires."

The beacons should have been lit!

"We've had no trouble for months from the foreigners. The sentries were lax. The barbarians approached in the dead of night and climbed the ladder to the signal towers before our men could climb up themselves. The watchmen were slain before any fires could be lighted."

"You're alone?" Quan asked. "The townsfolk are all dead or evacuated?"

"I don't know," the servant replied. "As I said, I haven't ventured outside for fear of the barbarians."

%%%

"Chains and witchery," Fong shouted. "The Pirate King has broken the truce!"

Li rushed outside to see her husband on the forecastle. It had taken her two hours to quiet the sickly boy and get him to close his eyes. Baby Lao was asleep in their quarters, and his father's shouting penetrated the thin walls and might awaken him at any moment.

"What is your problem?" Li called to him, and followed up the question by climbing the companionway to where he stood clenching his fists and sputtering like a frothing dog afflicted with the madness.

Fong met his wife with raging eyes. "Your pirate friends have raided a fleet of salt junks."

So, it had come to this. Mo Kuan-fu was not stupid and recognized an opportunity when it arose. The truce between Madam Choi and Admiral Fong meant that the Imperial Navy's hands were tied as long as the White Tiger depended upon the pirate woman to keep his wife and their newborn alive. In Fong's absence, the Pirate King had organized the pirate gangs into a confederation of thousands, which needed a dependable source of income to keep their loyalty. He had found it in the lucrative salt trade. Most salt fields were located near the sea, so the bulk of the freight was transported by junk. Each quarter, loaded fleets trekked the four thousand miles to Canton where their cargo was sold and distributed. Unbeknownst to Madam Choi, the pirates, under the command of Mo Kuan-fu, had sailed out of Chiang-ping with a fleet of three hundred junks and accosted the salt junks before they even left the harbour. While the salt itself was worth its weight in silver, the pirates were too lazy to sell it themselves, and instead, promised the merchants safe passage for a price.

A seaman whistled up to the forecastle and the sailor standing watch interrupted Admiral Fong. Apparently, one of the salt merchants had come aboard to make a complaint.

"We were promised safe seas by the Emperor. This shipment is vital to His Majesty's trade. If we do not reach our destination without the pirates making paupers of us, His Majesty will have our heads. Already, the merchants who have refused to pay protection money to the pirates have lost their cargo."

"Go back to your vessel," Fong ordered. "I will see that the problem is solved."

The merchant bowed and followed one of Fong's sailors to the main deck and then to the escort boat that had brought him aboard the warship.

Li narrowed her eyes suspiciously, studied her husband whose thoughts were masked behind his stolid expression. "What do you plan to do? You promised Madam Choi you would not attack them."

"I made no such promise. My promise was that I wouldn't attack *her*. And so I won't. I still need her for her doctoring skills, but I have no use for the one called Mo Kuan-fu, the Pirate King. Weigh anchor!" he shouted across the deck. "We set sail."

It took less than three day's voyage to negotiate the channel between the Lei-chou peninsula and Hainan Island. Once in the Gulf of Tonkin, an astonishing scene met their eyes: hundreds of armoured junks, their ragged bamboo sails raised against the morning sky and cannons cloaked on either side, crowded the harbour. Men stripped to the waist and faces shielded by wide straw hats, some with knotted kerchiefs around their necks, worked on the decks. Aboard one of the junks, a pirate lighted firecrackers to drive off evil spirits. This particular junk, Li could tell, had more than forty cannon, and was a large and splendid vessel, with a single black flag flying from its mainmast. It was one of the freight carriers of Kwangtung, stolen in the winter and converted into a pirate junk. Built of strong ironwood, it ran one hundred and fifty feet in length. Li knew it was of Kwangtung make because of the red bands in its hull, and now it was the flagship of the Black Flag fleet.

The pirates were obviously confident because of the size of the flotilla. No one was on watch, and Fong hove to and kept his warship out of sight. The Kwangtung junk, alone, was the size of his vessel. Capable of carrying four hundred men, it rode high in the water and would be difficult to board from sea. Fong ordered his Chief of Intelligence to the forecastle, paced the deck until the man arrived, then gave instructions for his people to infiltrate the pirates and learn exactly what target they intended to hit next.

"Let me go instead," Li interrupted.

Fong sighed. He had, after all, married a woman whose spunk was as big as her bite. When they returned to his cabin, Li insisted again on being the scout sent out to spy on the pirates. "They know me. They won't think I'm a spy. They know that Madam Choi is like a mother to me. I would never betray her."

"And yet what you propose to do is exactly that. You will betray them. I told you once before, Lotus Lily, I don't trust you."

"I'll betray *them*—for your sake, most honourable husband—but I won't betray *her*. She's not among them. We left her near Macao and only now will she realize that we are missing." She paused before adding, "If you prefer, I won't even allow them to see me. I'll disguise myself as a pirate, infiltrate their lair and learn their plot. Then I'll return to you my Supreme Lord Admiral."

Fong's Chief of Intelligence, a flat-eyed, yellow-faced man with large hands appeared at their opened doorway. He had overheard their disagreement and sided with Fong. "We cannot send your wife. She is one of them."

"No longer," Fong said. "She has vowed loyalty to me. I will take her at her word. She will blend in with the pirates. You on the other hand will stand out like a peeled lychee nut."

The Chief of Intelligence scowled, threw a black look at Li. "Mark my words," he began.

"Silence! I've made my decision." Fong turned to Li before dismissing his Chief of Intelligence. "You may go. Disguised. But keep low. Do not reveal your identity. Mo Kuan-fu cannot be trusted. Stories tell of his brutal and ruthless backstabbing. He would feed you to the sharks and feast on the shark's fin soup your body supplied before ever he placed another's need above his own. And if you double-cross me, your punishment will not be swift. It will be slow and tortuous."

Costumed in a torn jacket-like blouse and frayed black trousers made of a strong cheap fabric commonly used by the peasants for garments, Li roughened her face with grime and matted her hair into a lousy topknot. She kicked off her slippers and went barefoot, like the pirates of Madam Choi's fleet, and then slipped into a rowboat and rowed herself into the midst of the rogues and hoped that Captain Ching, also known as Mo Kuan-fu, would welcome her and take her into their pack.

The Kwangtung vessel belonged to him and she made her way directly there. Around her the bulk of the flotilla consisted of smaller craft, twin-masted junks of two hundred tons that carried less than a hundred and fifty men. These junks had distinct black and white hulls with fishing nets and ox hides draped over the sides to prevent boarding and to repel spears. There was also a convoy of river junks, and swarms of small rowboats that accompanied the fleets and squadrons with one or two sails and fourteen to twenty oars, and crews of eighteen to thirty men. These boats were long dragons, serpent boats and sampans. The sampans were especially well suited for fighting in shallow water or for mounting an on-shore attack. They had unmasted hulls with raised sterns that formed a platform on which the pilot and helmsman rode, and with a mat roof in the middle of the deck for shelter. Crewmembers and women alternated sculling while keeping watch.

Li passed into their midst unchecked. What was their target? When did they plan to attack? She crouched in her rowboat, beneath the massive red-banded hull of the Black Flag ship, and heard the answers to her questions unexpectedly when Mo Kuan-fu himself spoke from the deck above her head: "The target is a shipment of opium. A large fleet will pass the channel tonight. But they won't reach it if we have our way."

Something bumped her boat, and a fish knife slashed across her vision. A hand circled her chest from behind and tightened like sun-dried leather. "Struggle and you die like a spring lamb, sliced at the throat until your body is bled dry." Her assailant's boat double-bumped hers as he angled her face to his. "What do we have, here? A woman? I've not seen you before. What d'you think you're doing snooping on the Pirate King's private conversation?"

"May I speak?" Li croaked, darting a glance at the glistening knife, slick with seawater and traces of fish slime.

Her interrogator grappled her boat's gunwale with one hand while pinning her by the knife with the other. "Talk."

"My name is Li of Madam Choi's Red Flag Fleet. I've come with a proposition for your captain."

"What is this mysterious proposition?"

"My words are for Mo Kuan-fu's ears only."

The pirate wiped his snotty nose on his sleeve. His front teeth were missing and what remained was yellow. "Is that so? What makes you think he wants to hear what you have to say?"

"He knows me. He'll listen."

The snotty-nosed pirate snorted and the sound flapped out of his mucous-filled nostrils like a floundering fish's tail. A laugh from above them made Li snap her head up. "Captain Ching," she said.

The Pirate King squinted down from his ship and gave her a smarmy grin of recognition. "I know that brazen poppet. Haul her up. I want to speak with Madam Choi's adopted daughter."

The disgusting pirate accosting her reluctantly let go and Li sloughed off the repulsion of his touch, climbed the rope ladder and planted herself in Mo Kuan-fu's face. "Captain Ching," she said and bowed, "I am so pleased to see you again."

The pirate chief pursed his lips, studying her, but without returning the gesture or the sentiment. "I am called Mo Kuan-fu now," he corrected her.

"As you like." She bowed again.

His eyes slid up and down her raggedly dressed form, then landed on her dirt stained face. "Trouble in paradise?" he asked insolently.

She had to think quick, change tactics. "Admiral Fong is not involved with the mission I'm here to propose."

The pirate chief marched up and down the deck to annoy her. He spun on his heel. "What exactly do you propose? It is my understanding that you are already engaged in blissful wedlock." He smiled, but his eyes mocked. She could see his thoughts violating the sanctity of her marriage bed.

Li checked her disdain and the cutting insult that was itching to fly out of her mouth. "I am not looking for a pirate husband."

"Then what exactly are you looking for? Does your admiral know you're here?"

"He does. He sent me as a spy. Only he doesn't know

that I am about to betray him."

Mo Kuan-fu's expression creased with suspicion. "Go on."

She glanced at his companion who had been silent all this while, and he dismissed her concern with a flippant wave of his hand. "Meet my second in command. Hu Gow."

"Master Gow. This is a matter of confidentiality."

Mo Kuan-fu guffawed. "Confidentiality. Ha. There's no such thing among the water people. Now speak. Before I change my mind and feed you to the sharks."

"Fine. I need a ship and a crew to take me to the Yellow Sea. I intend to voyage to the Grand Canal and return to the Forbidden City, where I will find my son, whom the barbarian Esen has abducted." Before he could laugh at her or object, she continued, "You are a masterful rogue, a scourge of the seas. All who hear the name of the Pirate King tremble. The White Tiger has been brought to his knees by your rule over the South Coast waters. Even Madam Choi must concede to your greatness. But the barbarians are overrunning our country. Tell me, Mo Kuan-fu. Are you a traitor? Or are you Chinese?"

The pirate chief raised an eyebrow. "Are you calling me a traitor?"

"The boy I seek is the Emperor's grandson."

His eyes shot up. "That means you're the fugitive princess, Lotus Lily. What are you worth to the Emperor, I wonder?"

Li sucked on her lip. Either way, if he kept her hostage, if he took her to the Forbidden City, at least she'd be there. She'd figure out how to escape from him afterwards. "He will either treat you like a prince for returning the mother of his grandson or he will treat you like a prince for capturing the elusive Pirate Empress. Either way, it is a princely reception you will receive. My fate is of no consequence, only my son's matters. He must live to be the next ruler of China. If you help to rescue him, you'll be greatly rewarded."

Mo Kuan-fu frowned. "Haven't you heard? Since you married your foreign admiral, I have reaped many riches already. What could the Emperor grant me that I don't already have?"

"A pardon," Li said. "Absolution from your crimes against the Empire. Freedom to live your life any way you wish without a bounty on your head."

He smacked his lips like he had just tasted something delicious. "I like that, but just who is brave or skilled enough to capture the Pirate King?"

Li didn't answer. Mo Kuan-fu, if he accepted this proposal, would be tagged a wanted man. Admiral Fong would turn his hunt for the Pirate King into a personal vendetta.

"Are you afraid of the White Tiger?" Li taunted.

"Are you?" Mo Kuan-fu echoed.

%%%

Admiral Fong shouted his accusation loud enough for the heathen gods of all the ships in the pirate seas to hear. Madam Choi kept her dagger at hands reach. Po watched from the rigging, a crossbow aimed at the raving admiral. "She has betrayed me! She did not return from her foray amongst the pirates!"

"You were a fool to let her go."

The rage in Fong's eyes changed from red to white. His hand went to slap the impudent pirate woman, but her fist shot up clutching a blade that winked in the morning light, and he turned and paced the deck, Po's crossbow following his every step. Fong ordered his guards to stand down; he had no intention of harming Madam Choi or her children, but he would use them. For now he would let them go. He would send spies to follow her. Lotus Lily had abandoned her son—*his* son—and there was no forgiving that.

Fong sent a glance up to the rigging. Po had slackened his tension on the crossbow, but his wary eyes darted sharply.

"Your son will die without my medicines," Madam Choi said.

Fong was at a critical juncture. The pirate woman had him cornered. He couldn't travel the open seas with a sickly babe. He needed her and she knew it, and come hell or high water, she would never consent to travel with him and be his boy's nurse. Unless… could he take one of her children, the boy with the itchy bowhand perhaps? But how? Madam Choi was not without brains; she had stationed her son in the rigging long before he approached her ship.

He could have blown them out of the water for not consenting to come aboard his own vessel, but what would that accomplish? His only tie to Lotus Lily would be gone.

There must be another way. These ruffians had to sleep. But since his last altercation with Madam Choi her fleet had quadrupled. They no longer raided alone. There was always a vast flotilla surrounding her. He must buy time. His Majesty was sending his entire fleet to crush the pirates, and before they arrived, his reputation must be restored. Already word was out that the White Tiger had met his match. Never! He would never lose to a pirate, no less a female pirate.

CHAPTER FIFTEEN
The Rift and the Sinkhole

Po quietly poled the raft between Madam Choi's junk and the red-banded hull of Mo Kuan-fu. The sea sloshed over the bamboo logs, wetting his feet. He fastened a rope to the ladder running down from the deck, and clawed his way up from his raft. The knife between his teeth glinted in the moonlight. A haze surrounded the pale sphere of the moon, a thin funnel cloud dividing it into two. Po stuffed the knife into his boot. He wasn't going to need it and looked down to see how much of a trail he was leaving. Faint toe and heel prints darkened the wooden planks. The wind blew softly and it was only a matter of seconds before the evidence vanished. Po continued his trek. He knew the Pirate King's habits. The sloth was occupied with a woman after having stuffed himself with noodles and fried fish, and drunk himself stupid. Mo Kuan-fu would not be a hindrance tonight. The problem was: where to find Li?

Po suddenly caught sight of her. She was gambling with the best of them, seated on a crate in a circle of crates, and winning her share. A fight erupted between two drunkards, each accusing the other of cheating. Now was the time to attract her attention. Po slipped around behind the dueling twosome and nudged Li in the shoulder blade. She jerked up, her hands like cleavers ready to chop her assailant in half.

"It's me," he whispered from the shadows. "Don't draw attention this way!"

Li gasped, let her hands fall, glanced at the skirmish on deck that had now become an out and out brawl, capturing the attention of the entire crew. One of the brawlers grabbed the other by the throat and threatened to rip out his voice. Li gestured to Po to come around behind the bulkhead of the captain's cabin before she asked, "What are you doing here?"

"I'm here to ask you the same question. Admiral Fong is fit to explode. Why haven't you come back?"

"I was recognized. I took advantage of the opportunity to make a deal."

"The Pirate King's word is as good as a serpent's. He'll sell you out."

Li opened her mouth to object and Po shushed her by declaring, "Any bargain you made with him is worthless. Don't bother to explain. I know what bargain you made. He will take you to the Forbidden City, but not to find your son. He will sell you to the Emperor for an evil price."

"I know that," Li said. "But at least I'll be there."

"And what about your husband? He'll have your head if the Emperor doesn't slice it off first."

"That's a chance I'll have to take. I must find Wu ... Oh, don't give me that face, Po. Baby Lao is safe on board his father's warship. Wu is *not* safe. I must find him."

A sound came from inside the captain's cabin. "Come, it's not safe here. I have to get you off this junk before Mo Kuan-fu demands to know why you've come slinking aboard at night like a thief."

Li escorted Po across the deck, keeping to the shadows until they reached the side where he had boarded. They tripped over something soft, a body, and Li shook her head in contempt. Not only did Mo Kuan-fu violate his own rules about keeping faithful to his wife, but his crew saw all life as expendable. She sank to her knees to examine the corpse's face in the twilight and recognized it as one of the brawling crewmembers. Po touched the prone man's throat and noted that he was quite, irretrievably, dead. The rest of the crew had returned to the lantern-lit center deck, gone back to their drinking and gambling. The body would be disposed of in the morning when the pirates were sober.

Po descended the ladder, whispering up to Li, "What

message have you for Ma-ma?"

"No message. Except to flee Fong's side before the Emperor's fleet arrives to incarcerate you all."

%%%

Quan shouted at the top of his lungs, waving a frantic hand as he barged his way through a throng of horses and men readying for battle just inside the gates of the Forbidden City. He stopped in front of the military governor, swung his leg off his horse and dropped to the ground with a clatter of boots. "Altan is right behind me. It is only a matter of days before he gallops through the Juyong pass and takes the capital!"

Zheng Min thrust his head up from attending his horse. "Then what are you doing here? You should be holding him at Datong. Can't you see I have my hands full trying to muster reinforcements to drive Zi Shicheng and his rebels back from the northeast gates? He has joined forces with the Manchus and they are determined to breach the eastern wall."

Quan forced the tense muscles in his face to relax. "Where is His Majesty? Why isn't he out rallying the people himself?"

"He has called on the armies of Esen to help."

"What!"

"They've sealed a bargain: Esen's armies for the destruction of his brother and his forces. It will weaken the Mongol front. A house divided—"

Quan saw the logic instantly, but could they trust him? "Where is he?"

Zheng Min buckled his horse's saddle straps, yanked down his helmet and swung a leg over his mount without replying. Quan followed suit. There was no time to argue. If Esen could be taken at his word he would show up at the battlefield. If not... well, did Esen still have the power to recruit an army? And even if he did, how could he convince his warriors to destroy their own people? No, Quan would not gamble on the Mongol. He would rather bet on the courage of his own countrymen. The ragtag troops Zheng Min had managed to amass numbered in the tens of thousands, but would that be enough? He doubted it. He had seen the black tide of horsemen under Altan's command.

The *clip-clop* of hooves followed his lead. Out through the gates of the Forbidden City, they trotted into the deserted city accompanied by the rattle of drumrolls. Although the terrified citizens hid in their homes, Imperial protocol required the army announce their presence as they marched through the streets of Beijing. Quan had no choice but to submit to the convention. Once out in the bleak countryside, they abandoned all ceremony and raced to the hills, drums silent, and sped onward to the Dragon Wall that stretched across the horizon—a monument to Chinese supremacy—which was now more symbol than obstacle.

They navigated the pass with its dungeon-like battlements, capped with winged eaves overlooking the ragged coast of the Yellow Sea and the northern range. Scattering through the gate on the north side, Zheng Min's army came to a halt and assembled on the broad plain flanked by the illustrious mountain chain. In the distance Quan heard the clash of steel as the Manchus and the Chinese rebels ploughed through Ming soldiers.

Zheng Min stared in helpless disbelief as the idea of imminent defeat swamped him. "There is no hope. We are doomed."

"There is always hope," Quan retorted. "Steel yourself, man. Your men are watching."

Fifty thousand pairs of eyes waited nervously at attention while half that number of horses shuffled restlessly. Zheng Min's horse paced back and forth snorting puffs of frosty air, then rearing in protest, it whinnied and he reined it in. "You call these men?" he sneered. "They are farmers, labourers, merchants. Some of them are merely boys. They are not soldiers. A fortnight's training is not enough. They will fall dead from fear before an arrow ever pierces their hearts."

"Shut up," Quan said, and spat the acrid taste of dust from his mouth. "You are Military Governor, the top ranking officer of the Imperial Army. Act like it!"

Zheng Min scowled. "I am getting sick of you throwing your weight around, barking out orders. You want my job; I know it! You have been plotting it from the day you convinced His Majesty to build this infernal wall."

"Grapple your senses," Quan ordered, "before they take you to oblivion."

"Who are you to speak to me like that? Ever since you got your promotion you've been contradicting me in front of my men. I say we retreat. Blockade the walls of the city and, if worse comes to worse, seek sanctuary within the palace walls. We can fight them off from there."

"If we retreat, we are lost," Quan said.

"Then maybe it's time we realize that we cannot win this war. The prophesy of the Black Warrior of the North is true. He is a Manchu!"

"NO. We fight." Quan turned his back to the military governor, skimmed an eye over the disheveled lines of Ming forces and shouted, "Charge!"

The ragtag army flung themselves, crossbows taut, into the fray. The Manchus were crack marksmen; they had swiftness and accuracy on their side. The untrained soldiers of the Ming army rode into a stream of arrows like sitting ducks. Overhead, and from the opposite side, the buzz of ten thousand projectiles flew into the midst of the battling warriors. Quan wheeled his horse at the exact moment as Zheng Min who had stayed behind. They exchanged startled looks and, although they failed to see each other's eyes because of the distance, they knew the others' thought. Quan gaped at the rampaging Mongols who flew past him and flung themselves, C-bows strung, against the Manchus.

Were these Esen's men? He darted a frantic glance around but failed to locate the aging warlord.

A Manchu arrow pierced a Mongol horseman. So it was true. There was no love between them. No alliance. The Manchus had severed their Mongol ties and fought as a separate people. The battle was chaotic. Quan drew back uncertain as to who was fighting whom. He only knew that when the Ming fell—no matter where Esen's loyalties lay—the Mongols and the Manchus would battle it out to see who would gain the throne.

Quan had fought the Mongol invaders his entire military career. He refused to stand helplessly by while they claimed the Chinese throne. He wheeled his horse until he spotted the warlord Altan perched on his steppe horse, a fist in the air fitted with a falconer's glove. The golden fox pranced at his feet and before his eyes she transformed into the beautiful, dark-haired Jasmine.

"Not yet, barbarian!" Quan shouted. "The day is not taken!"

He lunged, his knees gripping his horse's flanks, his hands tight on his crossbow. He crossed the plain in a hare's breath, sweeping past Zheng Min, leaving him in dust. Behind, he heard the shuffle of horses hooves as an animal wheeled to follow. Was it Zheng Min? *Have you finally found your balls and are riding to my aid?*

An arrow bolt whistled past his ear just missing his back. Quan cranked his head sideways to get a look behind, and to spear the gutless Mongol. No Mongol was nearby. The barbarians had bypassed the Imperial Army, intending to take them out after destroying the Manchu threat. The only man within bow distance was Zheng Min, and he was aiming his crossbow at Quan's head. With sudden comprehension, Quan turned his horse. *The first projectile was intentional, meant to kill!* He reared his mount and took aim at Zheng Min's heart. He was about to let fly his arrow when a maelstrom of gold raced past him, whirling in ever decreasing circles.

In his confusion, Quan saw Zheng Min pause as the golden fox circled his horse as well. Faster and faster she flew in a dizzying figure eight, encompassing them both. Dust flew from her feet, her body transfigured into a red-gold projectile of soaring fur until a groundswell churned the earth into a gyro of spinning dirt. Zheng Min disappeared. The last thing Quan saw before his eyes blacked out was a shimmering tear in the atmosphere—that engulfed him.

%%%

"Where did they go?" Altan rode up to the fox as she cantered to a halt and blinked his eyes, but the two Ming champions were gone.

She stared into the settling dust filled with the pleasure and awe of her own power. Her long black hair flowed across her naked breasts as she resumed her human form, her snowy white gown flowing from her waist to the ground. She waved a hand in indifference and her sleeve flapped from her shoulder in the wind. "Where did they go?"

"Yes, woman. Where did they go?"

"I am not a woman. Don't call me one."

The veins in Altan's neck stood out like purple worms and his throat bobbed slightly. He narrowed his eyes before softening his look just a mote.

"I'll tell you where they went. One to the shadowland of Peng Lai and one to the Magpie Bridge called *Que Qiao*."

"Are they dead?"

"No, they are merely imprisoned for a time." Jasmine flashed her eyes at him, her annoyance abating, and blinked her lashes teasingly, lips curling into an impish smile. "They are gone, all right. But which went where?"

"Why did you do that? You should have let them kill each other. Then I could have taken the throne."

"With that at your gate? I don't think so." Jasmine flung

her hand in the direction of the frantic battle, and then looked sceptically at Altan. "Zi Shicheng has the Manchu army behind him. And rumours tell of Esen's return and he means to wipe you out. The Emperor has recruited him and he might just have enough clout to command a following. No, My Lord Warrior, Military Governor Zheng Min and Brigade General Chi Quan cannot die just yet; we still need them. When they've cooled down a bit, I'll return them to their posts."

The dust had settled completely. She drew in lusty swallows of the cold, crisp air. There was no evidence of what had transpired. The battle on the plain continued and the Ming soldiers fell one by one.

Here ends part two of THE PIRATE EMPRESS. *In part three,* **Azure Dragon**, *the Fox Faerie's magic has released an even greater evil, and Li's allies must fight new mythical forces before they can come to her aid.*

Acknowledgements

The idea for THE PIRATE EMPRESS came to me because of a long ago trip taken to China with my parents Dan and Stella Yee. There we walked the Great Wall of China, glimpsed the Ming tombs on the misty horizon, explored the excavated armies of First Emperor Qin and where I, as a Canadian, experienced my Chinese heritage for the first time. To my parents I am grateful for the insights I would not otherwise have had. My writing career has been a long and tenuous road, and I must thank those who helped me develop the courage and the tenacity to write such a lengthy novel. My gratitude goes out to Carolyn Niethammer, Robert Nielsen, Antanas Sileika, Kim Moritsugu and my late agent Joanne Kellock, whose suggestions and expertise helped make me the writer I am today. I am especially grateful to my former instructor Antanas Sileika, director of the Humber School for Writers, whose advice to follow my instincts has been an invaluable aid. Thank you to all of my fans and friends who have stuck by me through the years; a huge thanks to my husband whose support of this book is priceless. And thank you to that little Chinese man, who appeared in my dreams and my imagination, to tell me this story.

About the Author

Deborah Cannon grew up in Vancouver, British Columbia. Her fiction is inspired by her career as an archaeologist, which took her from Canada's west coast to England, the South Pacific Kingdom of Tonga and finally to the shores of Lake Ontario where she continues to be fascinated by myths, legends and cryptids.

In 2013 she won an honourable mention for her short story *Twilight Glyph* in the Canadian Tales of the Fantastic contest and in 2014 her story "Tang's Christmas Miracle" appeared in *Chicken Soup for the Soul: Christmas in Canada*. Her career as a science fiction/fantasy writer began when she sold two short stories to Farsector SFFH magazine (2003). She has contributed to the *Canadian Writer's Guide* and is best known for *The Raven Chronicles*, a series of paranormal archaeological suspense novels and a time slip series for young adults, *The Pirate Vortex*. Recently she launched a fiction series of Kindle Short Reads called *Close Encounters of the Cryptid Kind*. *The Pirate Empress* is her first Chinese epic fantasy.

She lives in Hamilton, Ontario with her archaeologist husband and two Shih-poos, working on future titles for these series.

Made in the USA
Monee, IL
21 June 2025

19775357R10098